#2
"INVASION"

THITAUME - SCRIPT

ROMAIN PUJOL - ART

GOROBEI - COLORIST

New York

ACKNOWLEDGEMENTS

Because they're all too often forgotten in favor of those who've brought their help and support, the authors would like to warmly thank all those who've absolutely nothing to do with the making of this volume:

Enzo Martin, Eva Bernard, Mathis Dubois, Lea Thomas, Ethan Robert, Louis Richard, Noah Petit, Louna Durand, Leo Leroy, Matheo More
Clement Simon, Maelys Laurent, Raphael Bertrand, Séverine Tallec, Lola Lefebvre, Maxime Michel, Nathan Garcia, Jules David, Arthur Re
Juliette Vincent, Tom Fournier, Lina Morel, Hugo Girard, Romane Andre, Pierre-André Bonnet, Max Perez, Benjamin Fournier, Anais Lefevre, T
Mercier, Alice Dupont, Clara Lambert, Yanis Bonnet, Mael Francois, Chloe Martinez, Adam Legrand, Jade Garnier, Camille Faure, Sarah Rousse
Lucie Blanc, Thomas Guerin, Louise Muller, Evan Henry, Lou Roussel, Paul Nicolas, Zoe Perrin, Lucas Morin, Timeo Mathieu, Lilou Clem
Ambre Gauthier, Nolan Dumont, Lisa Lopez, Axel Fontaine, Manon Chevalier, Gabriel Robin, Antoine Masson, Alexandre Sanchez, Cleme
Gerard, Noe Nguyen, Lena Boyer, Emma Denis, Ines Lemaire, Jeanne Duval, Louane Joly, Mathilde Gautier, Noa Roger, Sacha Roche, Bapt
Roy, Maxence Noel, Mohamed Meyer, Gabin Lucas, Alexis Meunier, Rayan Jean, Quentin Perez, Valentin Marchand, Mathys Dufour, Vic
Blanchard, Samuel Marie, Esteban Barbier, Kylian Brun, Martin Dumas, Romain Brunet, Simon Schmitt, Marie Tallec, Matteo Leroux, Aaron Co
Lorenzo Fernandez, Lenny Pierre, Bernard Louit, Robin Renard, Benjamin Arnaud, Adrien Rolland, Nael Caron, Liam Aubert, Pierre Giraud, Tito
Leclerc, Ilyes Vidal, Oceane Bourgeois, Charlotte Renaud, Marie Lemoine, Noemie Picard, Celia Gaillard, Anna Philippe, Nina Leclercq, Pau
Lacroix, Lana Fabre, Laura Dupuis, Lily Olivier, Ali Gator, Leonie Rodriguez, Alicia Da silva, Julie Hubert, Julia Louis, Rose Charles, Margaux Gui
Elise Riviere, Melina Le gall, Luna Guillaume, Elisa Adam, Sébastien Agostini, Margot Rey, Elsa Moulin, Maelle Gonzalez, Melissa Berger, Jus
Lecomte, Maeva Menard, Agathe Fleury, Elena Deschamps, Inaya Carpentier, Eliot Julien, Kevin Benoit, Morgan Paris, Nolann Maillard, Ibrat
Marchal, Elias Aubry, Moze Essame, Nolhan Vasseur, Sasha Le roux, Leandre Renault, Gaetan Jacquet, Ewen Collet, Alban Prevost, Hamza
irier, Matthieu Charpentier, Julian Royer, Alex Huet, Joshua Baron, Guillaume Dupuy, Nicolas Soustelle, Johan Pons, Tony Paul, Rayane Laine, L
Carre, Roland Martin, Milo Breton, Joseph Remy, Youssef Schneider, Yacine Perrot, Amir Guyot, Remi Barre, Pablo Marty, Mahe Cousin, Tess
goff, Alyssa Boucher, Angelina Bailly, Amelie Boulanger, Lucile Collin, Coline Herve, Clea Evrard, Lilia Poulain, Garance Etienne, Eleonore Lebi
Clarisse Daniel, Cédric Valéro, Bertrand Mathevon, Marie-Anne Passerel, Brian Xeira, Agu Lukke, Miguel Martin Collado, Nacho Hache, Af
Lopez, Samuel Peyric, Fanny Pereira, Selma Pasquier, Lily-rose Cordier, Sasha Humbert, Axelle Gillet, Solene Bouvier, Marwa Leveque, Flora
bert, Chiara Ferreira, Lucie Jorge, François Montagne, Laly Jacob, Nora Germain, Leila Klein, Roxane Millet, Alexia Weber, Eline Gomez, Ma
Marechal, Cassandre Gay, Maeline Chevallier, Hanae Mallet, Charly Lesage, Charlie Bertin, Gael Leblanc, Samy Alexandre, Teo Gonçalves, Zaka
Perrier, Aurelien Hamon, Naim Dos santos, Jeremy Rodrigues, Alain Tallec, Isaac Pelletier, Élie Coptère, Bilal Bouchet, Killian Monnier, Ali Lep
Owen Marin, Jordan Lemaitre, Lukas Reynaud, Ylan Pichon, Kyllian Lamy, Felix Antoine, Elouan Camus, Anis Georges, Mae Perret, Anas Coul
Thibaut Gros, Vincent Devaux, Ewan Langlois, Come Gilbert, Armand Tessier, Leandro Chauvin, Fares Ollivier, Lilly Levy, Salma Marion, Sir
Dupond, Anouk Joubert, Lili Jacques, Anissa Rossi, Lou-ann Besson, Rachel Legros, Camelia Guichard, Jules Belmer, Romain Mas, Daniel M'
Ariza, Violette Fernandes, Romy Carlier, Maelie Delattre, Iris Maury, Amina Cohen, Chaima Hernandez, Maely Guillon, Lou-anne Coste, Ja
Gargallo, Lya Verdier, Tessa Sauvage, Selena Lejeune, Sophie Martins, Charlie Ferrand, Carla Blanchet, Maryam Ruiz, Celeste Bousquet, Naor
Didier, Mia Tanguy, Melinda Michaud, Kelya Marques, Farah Gregoire, Milan Barthelemy, Adem Charrier, Bryan Briand, Achille Guillou, Ba
Maurice, Ilian Navarro, Damien Leduc, Lucien Pascal, Djibril Delorme, Lohan Delaunay, Justin Thibault, Romeo Bodin, Ahmed Valentin, Marv
Gaudin, Sami Allard, Melvin Mahe, Aymen Chauvet, Walid Masse, Marceau Tran, Sohan Vallee, Tim Barbe, Gregoire Buisson, Angelo Lebret
Gauthier Benard, Elliot Blondel, Yannis Laporte, Edouard Hebert, Nils Courtois, Aymeric Riou, Lois Legendre, Laurine Fischer, Maia Delannoy, Cla
Vaillant, Sana Lefort, Kelly Regnier, Noelie Guillet, Angele Couturier, Estelle Raynaud, Ema Bazin, Jean-René Lauzier, Ilona Bigot, Olivier Joya
Diane Peltier, Emeline Bourdon, Amelia Allain, Helena Descamps, Louisa Duhamel, Lara Dupre, Josephine Bruneau, Imane Besnard, Sere
Lenoir, Naila Lacombe, Louanne Laroche, Paloma Launay, Amel Loiseau, Asma Morvan, Fatima Jacquot, Maria Raymond, Magalie Gautier, Ne
Takagi, Alycia Rossignol, Jean Bonnaud, Alizee Auger, Aicha Brunel, Aurore Thierry, Nathael Jourdan, Celian Voisin, Jonathan Godard, Alan E
Yohan Baudry, Malone Pages, Joris Martel, Kilian Martineau, Emilien Faivre, Didier Reversat, Kelyan Berthelot, Fabio Pineau, Paolo Texier, Da
Girault, Andrea Normand, Michel Jorge, Etienne Petitjean, Elie Seguin, Clovis Blot, Roman Delmas, Eden Fouquet, Jason Guilbert, Matis Cc
Logan Merle, Leonard Pruvost, Mickael Labbe, Ismail Imbert, Abel Toussaint, Yoan Maillet, Ilhan Bonneau, Andy Tournier, Yoann Salaun, Cé
Leurent, Aurelle Montanger, Alexis Dorange, Nicolas Gallet, Thibault Juliard, Anaïs Poirier, Maelia Nicolay, Etoile Mercie, Noam Ben Reka
Narmane Ali, Kevin Bruhier Le Tallec, Hector Gallice, Ludovic Maillard, Marie-Laure Pourbaix, Roch De Labarthe, Pierre-Henry Mougenot, Rena
Pierre Carrot, Vivien Girard, Marine Hutinel, Léna Estebe, Franco Au Young, Simon Ghibaudo, Alexis Juville, Loic Muller, Laure Picard, Marie F
selier, Alexandra Vallet, Nelly Fournier, Lindsay Favre, Naomi Delage, Marco Renoux, Fatoumata Wagner, Eve Hardy, Daphne Gervais, Alb
Chretien, Jasmine Grandjean, Elodie Parent, Ella Gomes, Rania Peron, Kiara Guyon, Lilian Auget, Melody Lombard, Elia Claude, Shaina Clerc,
Chartier, Joèle Martin, Flavie Leblond, Lalie Lagarde, Syrine Da costa, Ava Guibert, Giulia Mace, Mayssa Leconte, Suzanne Chauveau, No
Prevot, Maelyne Hamel, Ilyana Cornu, Dounia Lelievre, Mariam Flament, Aliya Merlin, Christian Mallet, Melanie Vial, Emmanuel Boulay, Le
Bruneau, Martine Jorge, Monia Mechroub, Agathe Gehin, Iris De Soras, Tymeo Mary, Matthias Parmentier, Ange Valette, Emile Chapuis, Col
Balez, Aude Vanderschooten, Marianne De La Bruslerie, Joseph Biais, Lilian Fraisse, Evann Lecoq, Lino Mouton, Ilyas Geoffroy, Anatole Alves,
Ribeiro, Moussa Lopes, Bilel Laborde, Luc Besse, Max Marc, Mohammed Picot, Cameron Boutin, Jean Titouplin, Ulysse Lacoste, Wael Salm
Mohamed-amine Prigent, Alois Gilles, Tao Poisson, Marc Pujol, Anton Gallet, Soren Gueguen, Joachim Thiery, Jessy Lemonnier, Edgar Co
Lyam Serre, Vincent Chauvet, Idriss Bouvet, Nahil Foucher, Naelle Pottier, Coralie Mas, Wendy Grenier, Sophia Leonard, Esther Durant, Nes
Doucet, Jessica Potier, Perrine Torres, Clelia Le corre, Jean-Marie Philipp, Nicolas Thevenet, Alexandre Hartenstein, Cyrielle Ah-fa, Thomas Be
fils, Lin-Ly Chan, Thomas Wolter, Nicolas Moreau, Eloane Brault, Mathis Charbonnier, Lena Bouchard, Arthur Gras, Nathan Bayle, Noah Delaha
Axel Ferry, Eline Fraisse, Lilou Berthier, Lucie Maurin, Theo Bonhomme, Anais Bataille, Louna Bouquet, Jules Dubreuil, Lucas Lelong, Lisa Ra
Louis Prost, Timeo Duchemin, René Bruneau, Sandie Chrétienneau, Laëtitia Gomes, Pauline Le Guil, Pierre Petry, Charles Dupuis, Marion Depla
Hadrien Vercambre, Pauline Dillies, Paula Richeux, Matheo Jourdain, Clement Grand, Ambre Moreno, Maxime Bocquet, Enzo Lebon, Mar
Jacquemin, Ethan Neveu, Leo Becker, Yanis Husson, Arthur Soustelle, Léo Zapéra, Maelys Marquet, Raphael Combes, Romane Benoist, Anto
Guy, An-Khanh Le, Romain Gavache, Sébastien Carreli, François Essayan, Jonathan Ducoux, Lesly Benito, Lea Maire, Clemence Dumoulin, M
Huguet, Adam Bernier, Thomas Lafon, Nolan Sabatier, Juliette Rocher, Emmanuel Mota, Evan Arnould, Lola Boulet, Clara Lecocq, Tom Mora
Paul Ferre, Sophie Martin, Alice Comte, Hugo Monier, Sarah Le roy, Lou Thiebaut, Alexandre Bourdin, Eva Guillemin, Noe Leleu, Zoe Millot, Ir
Forestier, Jade Mangin, Emma Fortin, Lina Ricard, Camille Billard, Louise Le guen, Éric Constant, Gabriel Rousset, Chloe Jamet, Jeanne Roqu
Louane Chambon, Mathilde Jung, Noa Dujardin, Sacha Turpin, Baptiste Diaz, Maxence Prat, Mohamed Jolivet, Gabin Favier, Alexis Andrie
Rayan Castel, Quentin Bonnin, Valentin Ferrer, Mathys Grosjean, Victor Maurel, Kelly Diossi, Samuel Dias, Esteban Munoz, Kylian Chatelain, Ma
Rose, Romain Blondeau, Simon Guignard, Matteo Tellier, Aaron Cros, Lorenzo Le, Lenny Tardy, Robin Combe, Benjamin Cochet, Adrien Schm
Nael Magnier, Liam Sellier, Pierre Barreau, Titouan Monnet, Ilyes Guiraud, Oceane Zimmermann, Charlotte Granger, Marie Leon, Noemie Gac
Celia Andrieu, Anna Walter, Nina Granier, Jules Ferrand, Almir Auguste Girard, Marie Bertrand, Magdelayne Chapon, Jean Flatet, Elisabeth M
liner, Pauline Gosselin, Lana Drouet, Laura Villain, Lily Lavergne, Leonie Savary, Alicia Lagrange, Julie Faucher, Julia Fort, Rose Lafont, Marga
Grange, Elise Letellier, Melina Veron, Luna Bon, Elisa Lacour, Margot Vacher, Elsa Lecuyer, Maelle Guillemot, Melissa Lepage, Justine Guega
David Estragon Losada, Maeva Levasseur, Yohan Belkhiter, Rei Cool, Ben Thomas, Bilel Mhamdi, Caroline Iniesta, Chloé Vollmer-Lo, Marie Ro
mégoux, Agathe Armand, Elena Bonnefoy, Inaya Keller, Eliot Derrien, Kevin Le bihan, Claire Silvestre-Knopf , Denis Gagniere, Noémie Chi

Léopold Bensaid, Jordan Pelluard, Adeline Caillon, Morgan Samson, Nolann Geffroy, Ibrahim Mignot, Elias Prieur, Nolhan Le borgne, Sasha Delaporte, Martin Bustarret, Monique Peyric, Leandre Poncet, Gaetan Belin, Ewen Le gal, Alban Kieffer, Hamza Bonnard, Matthieu Gil, Julian Blaise, Alex Mounier, Joshua Vernet, Guillaume Baudouin, Johan Bob, Tony Laval, Rayane Duclos, Loic Hoffmann, Milo Lefranc, Joseph Godefroy, Youssef Payet, Yacine Lalanne, Amir Corre, Remi Rigaud, Pablo Caillaud, Mahe Le bras, Tess Jeanne, Alyssa Berard, Angelina Morice, Amelie Cartier, Lucile Tisserand, Coline Saunier, Clea Weiss, Lilia Pommier, Garance Gallois, Eleonore Stephan, Clarisse Bauer, Fanny Ramos, Selma Villette, Sophie Colson, Lily-rose Lavigne, Sasha Casanova, Axelle Beck, Solene Guitton, Marwa George, Flora Ledoux, Chiara Dupin, Laly Cornet, Nora Brossard, Marion Orsucci, Leila Bureau, Roxane Maitre, Lara Tatouille, Alexia Desbois, Eline Vannier, Mailys Sergent, Cassandre Papin, Maeline Constant, Hanae Lallemand, Charly Claudel, Charlie Marcel, Gael Martinet, Samy Lemarchand, Teo Pinto, Zakaria Jouan, Aurelien Simonnet, Naim Barret, Jeremy Demange, Isaac Pierron, Bilal Soler, Killian Maillot, Ali Bastien, Owen Mathis, Jordan Vigneron, Lukas Quere, Ylan Poirot, Kyllian Berthet, Felix Terrier, Elouan Bellanger, Anis Sicard, Mae Leray, Anas Gicquel, Thibaut Roland, Vincent Jarry, Ewan Lang, Come Tavernier, Armand Jullien, Mothy Richard, Noé Garcia, Matthew Charlton, Justine Tardy, Maria la Bretonne, Maxime Paka, Leandro Le berre, Francis Capelle, those who read this text, Lilly Thebault, Salma Bois, Sirine De sousa, Anouk Joseph, Lili Vivier, Anissa Foulon, Lou-ann Janin, Rachel Chevrier, Camelia Nicolle, Anaïs Bligait, Pierre-Alexandre Juge, Pierre Roussel, Sidonie Bardet, Christine Pham, Nicolas Jesson, Emilie Pineau, Concetta Galani, Allison Lamarre, Clémentine Goutaine, Cécilia Brahmi, Sandrine Penet, Marina Narishkin, Daravong Saravong, Amélia Ducasse, Victor Dookie, Pascal Yan, Charles Nouveau, Romy Sentrie, Jean-Michel Rosenblat, Laura Popee, Guillaume Fleur, Violette De oliveira, Romy Aubin, Maelie Payen, Iris Ragot, Amina Esnault, Chaima Louvet, Maely Hamelin, Lou-anne Jan, Lya Binet, Tessa Champion, Selena Galland, Sophie Chene, Charlie Forest, Carla Pinel, Maryam Caillet, Celeste Goujon, Naomie Fayolle, Mia Thery, Melinda Latour, Kelya Sarrazin, Farah Proust, Milan Froment, Adem Lebeau, Bryan Viard, Achille Portier, Léna Tallec, Vincent Zapéra, Basile Deshayes, Ilian Alix, Damien Langlais, Lucien Gibert, Pierre Reversat, Djibril Marteau, Lohan Dubus, Justin Brochard, Romeo Courtin, Ahmed Gimenez, Marwan Lefeuvre, Sami Ly, Melvin Felix, Basile Dumez, Aymen Lefrancois, Walid Larcher, Marceau Mora, Sohan Piquet, Tim Baudin, Gregoire Alvarez, Angelo Devos, Gauthier Lasserre, Elliot Mendes, Yannis Romain, Caroline Martin, Edouard Chollet, Nils Marais, Aymeric Foucault, Lois Godet, Laurine Durieux, Maia Chateau, Claire Duprat, Sana Charlot, Kelly Jegou, Noelie Esteve, Angele Jolly, Estelle Le floch, Ema Collignon, Ilona Bossard, Diane Beaufils, Emeline Duchene, Amelia Billet, Helena Pasquet, Louisa Allemand, Lara Teixeira, Josephine Villeneuve, Imane Tissier, Serena Vilain, Naila Tison, Louanne Roth, Sarah Suhr, Clémence Breuil, Paloma Bailleul, Amel Parisot, Asma Fourcade, Fatima Serra, Maria Briere, Alycia Bouche, Alizee Moine, Aicha Lienard, Aurore Magne, Timothy Wachs, Nathael Salomon, Celian Romero, Jonathan Leclere, Alan Lapierre, Yohan Rio, Malone Simonin, Joris Cariou, Kilian Jouve, Emilien Basset, Kelyan Blandin, Fabio Lallement, Paolo Garreau, Daniel Guilbaud, Andrea Hue, Etienne Chabert, Elie Gobert, Lilou Gargallo, Clovis Darras, Roman Beaumont, Eden Rivet, Jason Duchesne, Matis Raynal, Logan Provost, Leonard Berthe, Mickael Guillard, Ismail Boudet, Abel Verrier, Yoan Pollet, Ilhan Delarue, Andy Carriere, Yoann Teyssier, Alexandra Charlet, Lindsay Boivin, Matthias Barabinot, Albany Petrouhka, Kassem Messak, Louis Roy, Thibaud Cassan, Donald Logeais, Morgane Tison, Quentin Heroguer, Camille Froehlicher, Guillaume Penchinat, Thomas Marie, Sarah Commerman, Florian Maurette, Heidi Etcheverry, Valéry Dupouet, Pascale Skeene, Jérémy Binet, Clélia Ka, Cécile Pouyet, Pauline Silvestre, Ophélie Galmiche, Naomi Senechal, Fatoumata Thevenin, Eve Soulie, Daphne Jaouen, Albane Pinson, Marie Mulot, Jasmine Crepin, Elodie Rougier, Ella Nogues, Rania Bonin, Kiara Viaud, Melody Legay, Elia Peres, Stéphane Poutet, Shaina Bordes, Ana Abadie, Flavie Magnin, Lalie Baudoin, Syrine Tissot, Ava Cardon, Giulia Lassalle, Mayssa Poulet, Suzanne Bour, Norah Michon, Maelyne Puech, Ilyana Baudet, Dounia Mille, Mariam Porte, Aliya Bourbon, Melanie Ducrocq, Marc Vador, Emmanuel Le meur, Tymeo Bourgoin, Matthias Le breton, Ange Le bris, Emile Gasnier, Erwann Serrano, Lino Soulier, Ilyas Bourguignon, Anatole Calvez, Elio Charlier, Moussa Mahieu, Bilel Jacquin, Luc Pouget, Max Villard, Mohammed Perin, Cameron Pichard, Sandy Jaunet, Ulysse Pernot, Wael Cottin, Mohamed-amine Arnoux, Alois Rigal, Tao Crouzet, Marc Moi, Anton Gosset, Soren Reboul, Joachim Ben, Jessy Lesueur, Edgar Pires, Anna-Lise Durine, Lyam Peyre, Idriss Schwartz, Nahil Loisel, Naelle Boutet, Coralie Landais, Wendy Rodier, Sophia Duquesne, Esther Peter, Nesrine Page, Jessica Lamotte, Perrine Babin, Clelia Thuillier, Eloane Genin, Noe Le roy, Evan Le gal, Gabriel David, Emma Faure, Anais Fontaine, Lilou Lemaire, Maelys Marie, Matheo Caron, Lucie Fabre, Theo Guillaume, Noah Adam, Lina Gonzalez, Maxime Deschamps, Louis Paris, Juliette Renault, Jade Baron, Ambre Laine, Yann Baffalio, Lea Carre, Clement Barre, Clemence Marty, Ines Jacob, Lena Hamon, Dadaï Malhaire, Lola Marin, Eva Camus, Mathis Maury, Paul Navarro, Hugo Thibault, Leo Masse, Nathan Barbe, Raphael Bazin, Manon Descamps, Louna Duhamel, Alice Pages, Lou Girault, Zoe Labbe, Timeo Toussaint, Romane Favre, Lucas Hardy, Nolan Claude, Clara Lagarde, Chloe Hamel, Sarah Brault, Yanis Bayle, Enzo Rault, Alexandre Maire, Lisa Lafon, Axel Jamet, Jules Tardy, Ethan Lagrange, Tom Grange, Camille Blaise, Mael Laval, Antoine Payet, Adam Lalanne, Thomas Jeanne, Louise Bauer, Arthur Ramos, Jeanne Papin, Louane Demange, Mathilde Jarry, Noa Thebault, Sacha Janin, Baptiste Payen, Maxence Ragot, Mohamed Esnault, Elodie Doret, Gabin Sarrazin, Camille Garcia, Mana Aandreu, Jean-Baptiste Cazes, Émilien Pigrais, Mathilde Bellec, Karl Grux, Guillaume Golay, Louis Curié, Ryū–ku Ushio, Pierre Courtina, Joëlle Barbier, Yannick Lejeune, Sylvain Beyer, Tess Excoffier, Mohamed Khalef, Ibrahim Berro, Elrik Villon-Pinel, Sarah Januel, Lucie Lépine, Bilel Mhamdi, Mélisande Leilos, Julie Pérocheau, Virginie Siveton, Fabien Duchene, Joe Skull, Ben Thomas, Victorien Boutteau, Adrien Spada, Mono' Aloïs Elbahjaoui, Charlotte Guibé, Mélisande Leilos, Antoine Barthe, Pierre Courtina, Mathilde Buron, Benoit Bekaert, Matthias Barabinot, Marc Monge, Ben Thomas, Anne-lise Nalin, Sylvain Maupin, Cécile McMillan, Stivo Chopin, Alexis Deshayes, Rayan Alix, Quentin Alvarez, Valentin Foucault, Mathys Magne, Bob-Garry Callaghan Batte, Victor Delarue, Maelle Tallec, Monique Poitevin, Samuel Abadie, Esteban Lassalle, Kylian Schwartz, Martin Babin, Romain Dubois, Simon Robert, Matteo Lefebvre, Aaron Lambert, Lorenzo Barbier, Lenny Brun, Robin Aubert, Benjamin Hubert, Adrien Lebrun, Nael Humbert, Liam Albert, Pierre Gilbert, Titouan Joubert, Ilyes Hebert, Oceane Blin, Charlotte Blot, Mo Malhaire, Marie Guilbert, Noemie Imbert, Celia Lombard, Anna Guibert, Nina Thiebaut, Pauline Bon, Lana Bob, Laura Le bras, Lily Beck, Leonie Desbois, Alicia Bois, Julie Lebeau, Julia Gibert, Rose Guilbaud, Margaux Chabert, Elise Gobert, Melina Bour, Luna Le bris, Elisa Reboul, Nicole Hacquard, Margot Ben, Elsa Michel, Maelle Vincent, Melissa Mercier, Justine Francois, Maeva Sanchez, Agathe Picard, Elena Marchal, Inaya Boucher, Eliot Marechal, Kevin Bouchet, Morgan Pichon, Nolann Blanchet, Ibrahim Fischer, Elias Foucher, Nolhan Becker, Sasha Rocher, Leandre Lecocq, Gaetan Ricard, Ewen Cros, Felipe Barris, Alban Cochet, Hamza Faucher, Gérard Menvussat, Matthieu Lacour, Julian Vacher, Alex Duclos, Joshua Sicard, Guillaume Lefrancois, Johan Larcher, Tony Fourcade, Rayane Senechal, Loic Michon, Milo Cordier, Joseph Verdier, Youssef Didier, Yacine Godard, Amir Jourdain, Remi Diaz, Pablo Dias, Mahe Blondeau, Tess Ledoux, Alyssa Baudoin, Angelina Landais, Amelie Rodier, Lucile Petit, Coline Leroy, Clea Lefevre, Lilia Guerin, Garance Henry, Eleonore Denis, Clarisse Meyer, Fanny Perez, Selma Pierre, Lily-rose Bourgeois, Sasha Leclercq, Axelle Fleury, Solene Breton, Marwa Herve, Flora Etienne, Ethan Tallec, Catherine Aloccio, Chiara Pereira, Laly Leveque, Nora Ferreira, Leila Weber, Roxane Leger, Alexia Lejeune, Eline Leduc, Mailys Lebreton, Cassandre Thierry, Maeline Berthelot, Hanae Merle, Charly Peron, Charlie Prevot, Gael Lelievre, Samy Valette, Teo Lecoq, Zakaria Ribeiro, Aurelien Besse, Naim Serre, Jeremy Ferry, Isaac Dubreuil, Bilal Duchemin, Killian Lebon, Ali Jacquemin, Owen Neveu, Jordan Ferre, Lukas Guillemin, Ylan Leleu, Kyllian Gosselin, Felix Veron, Elouan Guillemot, Anis Guegan, Mae Bonnefoy, Anas Belin, Thibaut Weiss, Vincent Villette, Ewan Vigneron, Come Leray, Armand Le berre, Leandro Capelle, Fares De oliveira, Lilly Hamelin, Salma Gimenez, Sirine Felix, Anouk Devos, Lili Lasserre, Anissa Jegou, Lou-ann Teixeira, Rachel Villeneuve, Camelia Serra, Violette Lapierre, Romy Duchesne, Maelie Thevenin, Iris Crepin, Amina Legay, Chaima Peres, Maely Le breton, Lou-anne Perin, Lya Peyre, Tessa Duquesne, Selena Peter, Sophie Genin, Charlie Dufour, Carla Lefort, Maryam Geffroy, Celeste Fort, Naomie Lafont, Mia Geffroy, Melinda Kieffer, Kelya Godefroy, Farah Beaufils, Milan Rodriguez, Adem Le gall, Bryan Le goff, Achille Gay, Basile Rodrigues, Ilian Gros, Damien Legros, Lucien Rossignol, Djibril Seguin, Lohan Wagner, Justin Prigent, Romeo Gueguen, Ahmed Gras, Marwan Guy, Sami Huguet, Melvin Le guen, Aymen Mignot, Walid Gil, Marceau Rigaud, Sohan Sergent, Tim Collignon, Gregoire Rougier, Angelo Nogues, Gauthier Magnin, Elliot Bourgoin, Yannis Bourguignon, Edouard Richard, Nils Mathieu, Aymeric Gauthier, Lois Marchand, Laurine Blanchard, Maia Huet, Claire Guichard, Sana Michaud, Kelly Bouchard, Noelie Delahaye, Guillaume Clavery, Angele Berthier, Estelle Lemarchand, Ema Chene, Ilona Thery, Diane Brochard, Emeline Duchene, Amelia Hue, Helena Mahieu, Louisa Pichard, Lara Simon, Josephine Martinez, Imane Vidal, Fix Germain, Vincent Crevillard, Serena Philippe, Naila Da silva, Louanne Riviere, Paloma Schneider, Amel Bailly, Asma Lemaitre, Fatima Briand, Maria Bigot, Alycia Voisin, Alizee Faivre, Aicha Picot, Aurore Thiery, Nathael Bataille, Celian Jolivet, Jonathan Andrieux, Alan Le bihan, Yohan Prieur, Malone Lavigne, Joris Maitre, Kilian Martinet, Emilien Pinto, Kelyan Poirot, Fabio Binet, Paolo Pinel, Daniel Viard, Andrea Durieux, Etienne Tison, Elie Parisot, Clovis Briere, Roman Rivet, Eden Carriere, Jason Boivin, Matis Viaud, Logan Mille, Leonard Rigal, Mickael Pires, Ismail Loisel, Jean-Luc

Berton, Abel Joly, Yoan Jean, Ilhan Petitjean, Andy Grandjean, Yoann Jung, Alexandra Grosjean, Lindsay Jan, Naomi Blanc, Fatoumata Muller, Eve Chevalier, Daphne Rolland, Albane Leclerc, Jasmine Gaillard, Elodie Guillot, Ella Julien, Rania Maillard, Kiara Collet, Pauline Peyric, André Bouty, Melody Collin, Sandrine Fiches, Elia Poulain, Shaina Gillet, Ana Klein, Flavie Millet, Lalie Chevallier, Syrine Mallet, Ava Leblanc, Giulia Gonçalves, Mayssa Lamy, Suzanne Langlois, Norah Levy, Maelyne Carlier, Ilyana Guillon, Dounia Barthelemy, Mariam Guillou, Aliya Allard, Melanie Vallee, Emmanuel Vaillant, Tymeo Guillet, Matthias Allain, Ange Delmas, Emile Maillet, Evann Salaun, Lino Vallet, Ilyas Delage, Anatole Clerc, Elio Leblond, Moussa Alves, Bilel Salmon, Luc Gilles, Max Gallet, Mohammed Lelong, Cameron Millot, Ulysse Billard, Wael Chatelain, Mathieu Rébois, Mohamed-amine Tellier, Alois Le, Tao Sellier, Marc Leon, Anton Walter, Soren Villain, Joachim Letellier, Jessy Keller, Edgar Caillaud, Lyam Gallois, Idriss Maillot, Nahil Roland, Naelle Lang, Coralie Jullien, Wendy Galland, Sophia Caillet, Esther Langlais, Nesrine Ly, Ubert Senzash, Jessica Chollet, Pierre Kiroul, Perrine Le floch, Clelia Billet, Eloane Vilain, Eva Bailleul, Adam Leclere, Lilou Guillard, Lina Pollet, Zoe Soulier, Ambre Calvez, Manon Charlier, Matheo Villard, Yaz Bouchara, Louna Thuillier, Lucas Clement, Enzo Dumont, Benjamin Gargallo, Lisa Schmitt, Clement Germain, Leo Mahe, Clara Raymond, Lena Normand, Romane Mace, Anais Flament, Clemence Mary, Margaux Malhaire, Lucie Marc, Louis Mas, Alice Combes, Noe Chambon, Hugo Schmidt, Juliette Zimmermann, Thomas Armand, Lou Samson, Jules Hoffmann, Gabriel Pommier, Tom Lallemand, Alexandre Froment, Lola Mora, Camille Romain, Sarah Allemand, Chloe Romero, Timeo Lallement, Jade Beaumont, Ethan Le meur, Evan Moi, Ines Bernard, Antoine Fournier, Maelys Andre, Nathan Bonnet, Mathis Garnier, Axel Noel, Louise Meunier, Paul Fernandez, Arthur Renard, Raphael Arnaud, Noah Renaud, Emma Menard, Maxime Benoit, Nolan Boulanger, Yanis Daniel, Mael Alexandre, Lea Dos santos, Theo Monnier, Jeanne Reynaud, Louane Fernandes, Mathilde Hernandez, Noa Tanguy, Sacha Valentin, Baptiste Benard, Maxence Blondel, Mohamed Legendre, Gabin Delannoy, Alexis Regnier, Rayan Raynaud, Quentin Bruneau, Valentin Besnard, Mathys Lenoir, Victor Martineau, Samuel Pineau, Xavier Crabe, Esteban Bonneau, Kylian Tournier, Martin Lemonnier, Romain Grenier, Simon Leonard, Matteo Charbonnier, Aaron Bernier, Lorenzo Monier, Lenny Mangin, Robin Bonnin, Benjamin Guignard, Adrien Magnier, Nael Monnet, Liam Granger, Pierre Granier, Titouan Poncet, Ilyes Bonnard, Oceane Mounier, Charlotte Saunier, Marie Casanova, Noemie Vannier, Celia Simonnet, Anna Bellanger, Julien Aloccio, Nina Tavernier, Pauline Mendes, Lana Lienard, Laura Blandin, Lily Pinson, Fabien Baffalio, Leonie Gasnier, Alicia Arnoux, Julie Thomas, Julia Morel, Rose Nicolas, Margaux Morin, Elise Lopez, Melina Robin, Luna Boyer, Elisa Roger, Margot Roche, Elsa Colin, Maelle Lemoine, Melissa Louis, Justine Lecomte, Maeva Royer, Agathe Gomez, Elena Antoine, Inaya Rossi, Eliot Cohen, Kevin Coste, Morgan Gregoire, Nolann Delorme, Ibrahim Bodin, Elias Laporte, Nolhan Lacombe, Sasha Laroche, Leandre Colas, Gaetan Gomes, Ewen Da costa, Alban Leconte, Hamza Cornu, Matthieu Lopes, Julian Laborde, Alex Lacoste, Joshua Costa, Guillaume Le corre, Johan Bonhomme, Tony Benoist, Rayane Arnould, Loic Comte, Milo Combe, Joseph Godin, Youssef Drouet, Jérôme Brizard, Yacine Delaporte, Amir Baudouin, Remi Corre, Pablo George, Michael Delouis, Mahe Jouan, Tess Soler, Alyssa De sousa, Angelina Nicolle, Amelie Fayolle, Lucile Proust, Coline Godet, Clea Jolly, Lilia Moine, Garance Salomon, Eleonore Simonin, Clarisse Jouve, Edouard Hache, Fanny Jaouen, Selma Bonin, Lily-rose Porte, Sasha Lamotte, Axelle Dupont, Solene Dupuis, Marwa Pons, Flora Paul, Chiara Dupond, Laly Chapuis, Nora Prat, Leila Lepage, Roxane Stephan, Alexia Champion, Eline Duprat, Mailys Page, Cassandre Jacquet, Maeline Jacques, Hanae Bousquet, Charly Marques, Charlie Jacquot, Gael Fouquet, Samy Bouquet, Teo Bocquet, Arthur Colin, Raoul Paoli, Kassem Messak, Jérémy Binet, Sarah Commerman, Anton Roux, Vincent Lévêque, Arnaud Bonadei, Patrice Boudier, Romy Sentrie, Yohan Sacré, Raul Blogue, Julian Promo, Yoann Chevallier, Victor Dookie, Mathilde Bellec, Karl Grux, Nicolas Hasseler, David Fauster, Thibaud Cassan, Sylvain Beyer, Guillaume Coulin, Cécile Jocteur, Javier Blankovitch, Mayline Tomasi Rakotomalala, Lucie Rouillay, Louis Roy, Alexis Tison, Claire Pigrais, Léa Pichot, Pierre Roussel, Zakaria Marquet, Aurelien Roques, Naim Gicquel, Jeremy Piquet, Mégan Balez, Isaac Pasquet, Bilal Jacquin, Killian Martin, Ali Durand, Owen Moreau, Jordan Laurent, Lukas Garcia, Ylan Bertrand, Kyllian Roux, Felix Girard, Elouan Legrand, Anis Perrin, Mae Gerard, Anas Roy, Thibaut Leroux, Vincent Giraud, Ewan Lacroix, Médhi Khaman, Come Charles, Armand Rey, Leandro Berger, Fares Le roux, Lilly Poirier, Salma Remy, Sirine Perrot, Anora Costigan, Anouk Evrard, Lili Bertin, Anissa Perrier, Lou-ann Georges, Rachel Perret, Camelia Marion, Violette Ferrand, Romy Ruiz, Maelie Charrier, Iris Maurice, Amina Riou, Chaima Couturier, Maely Bourdon, Paul Pelade, Lou-anne Morvan, Lya Jourdan, Tessa Martel, Selena Parent, Sophie Merlin, Charlie Durant, Carla Torres, Maryam Prost, Celeste Grand, Naomie Moreno, Mia Morand, Melinda Bourdin, Kelya Fortin, Farah Dujardin, Milan Turpin, Adem Ferrer, Bryan Rose, Marc Peyric, Achille Barreau, Basile Guiraud, Ilian Andrieu, Damien Lavergne, Lucien Derrien, Djibril Le borgne, Lohan Vernet, Justin Lefranc, Romeo Berard, Ahmed Morice, Marwan Tisserand, Sami Cornet, Melvin Bureau, Aymen Marcel, Walid Barret, Marceau Pierron, Sohan Terrier, Tim Chevrier, Gregoire Forest, Angelo Courtin, Gauthier Marais, Elliot Charlot, Yannis Roth, Edouard Rio, Nils Cariou, Aymeric Garreau, Lois Darras, Laurine Berthe, Maia Verrier, Claire Charlet, Sana Bordes, Kelly Cardon, Noelie Bourbon, Angele Ducrocq, Estelle Serrano, Ema Pernot, Ilona Rousseau, Diane Roussel, Emeline Masson, Amelia Vasseur, Helena Lesage, Louisa Tessier, Sess Boudebesse, David Dartois, Céline Dartois, Jean-François Baissac, Julien Fau, Brice Martigné, Jérôme Bedos, Sabine André, Benjamin Mazoyer, Romain Leze, Jérôme Guirassevich Nicolas Sévenier, Nicolas Escamilla, Lara Besson, Josephine Pascal, Imane Buisson, Serena Loiseau, Naila Poisson, Aymeric Jaunet, Louanne Husson, Paloma Rousset, Amel Castel, Asma Levasseur, Fatima Brossard, Maria Joseph, Alycia Bossard, Alizee Tissier, Aicha Basset, Aurore Teyssier, Nathael Tissot, Celian Gosset, Jonathan Gautier, Alan Carpentier, Faustine Gargallo, Yohan Charpentier, Malone Pelletier, Joris Delattre, Kilian Martins, Emilien Tran, Kelyan Courtois, Fabio Peltier, Paolo Chretien, Daniel Chartier, Andrea Parmentier, Etienne Pottier, Elie Potier, Clovis Sabatier, Roman Forestier, Eden Cartier, Jason Guitton, Matis Constant, Logan Bastien, Leonard Mathis, Mickael Berthet, Ismail Latour, Abel Portier, Yoan Marteau, Ilhan Chateau, Andy Esteve, Yoann Cottin, Alexandra Nguyen, Lindsay Duval, Naomi Lucas, Fatoumata Dumas, Eve Brunet, Daphne Moulin, Albane Aubry, Jasmine Dupuy, Elodie Guyot, Ella Cousin, Rania Pasquier, Kiara Coulon, Melody Chauvin, Elia Delaunay, Shaina Gaudin, Ana Chauvet, Flavie Dupre, Lalie Launay, Syrine Auger, Fabien Auberger, Ava Brunel, Giulia Baudry, Mayssa Guyon, Suzanne Boulay, Norah Mouton, Maelyne Boutin, Ilyana Pujol, Dounia Bouvet, Mariam Doucet, Nico Pigrais, Aliya Maurin, Melanie Dumoulin, Erwan Jaunet, Emmanuel Boulet, Tymeo Maurel, Matthias Munoz, Ange Lecuyer, Emile Dupin, Evann Claudel, Lino Quere, Ilyas Foulon, Alexandre Escamilla, Olivier Vidal, Landry Giambra, Étienne Bonnet, Anatole Aubin, Elio Louvet, Moussa Goujon, Bilel Dubus, Luc Lefeuvre, Max Baudin, Damien Le Guerroué, Mohammed Bouche, Cameron Boudet, Ulysse Soulie, Wael Poulet, Mohamed-amine Puech, Alois Baudet, Tao Pouget, Marc Crouzet, Anton Lesueur, Soren Boutet, Joachim Olivier, Jessy Prevost, Edgar Bouvier, Lyam Devaux, Idriss Ollivier, Nahil Sauvage, Naelle Pruvost, Coralie Gervais, Wendy Chauveau, Sophia Vial, Esther Favier, Nesrine Savary, Jessica Vivier, Perrine Provost, Clelia Texier, Eloane Raynal et Jalil Essalihi.

RABBIDS #2 "INVASION"
Thitaume – Writer
Romain Pujol – Artist
Gorobei – Colorist
Joe Johnson – Translator
Jeff Whitman – Production Coordinator
Michael Petranek – Production and Associate Editor

Jim Salicrup
Editor-in-Chief

978-1-62991-159-5 Paperback Edition
978-1-62991-160-1 Hardcover Edition

Papercutz books may be purchased for business or promotional use. For information on bulk purchases please contact Macmillan Corporate and Premium Sales Department at (800) 221-7945 x5442.

PRINTED IN CHINA
MARCH 2015 By WKT CO. LTD.
3/F PHASE I LEADER INDUSTRIAL CENTRE
188 TEXACO, TSUEN WAN, N.T., HONG KONG

DISTRIBUTED BY MACMILLAN
FIRST PAPERCUTZ PRINTING

THE BIG BONUS GAME

THE AUTHORS HAD FUN HIDING VARIOUS OBJECTS THROUGHOUT THIS GRAPHIC NOVEL:

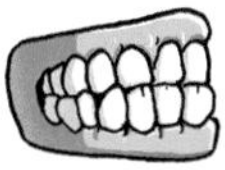

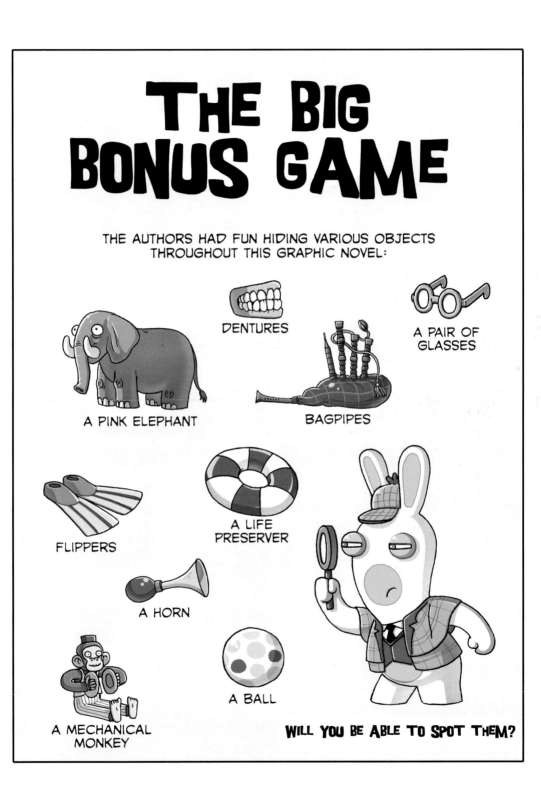

DENTURES

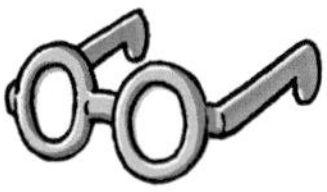

A PAIR OF GLASSES

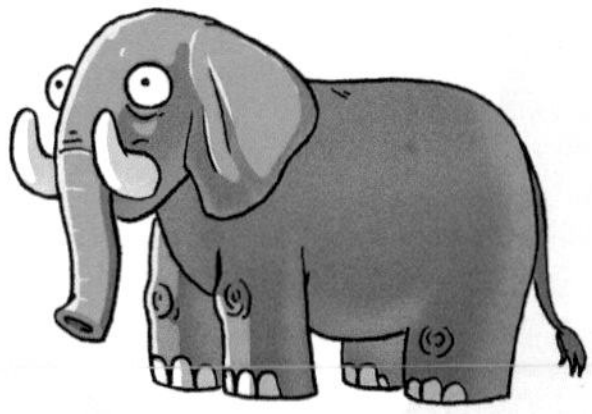

A PINK ELEPHANT

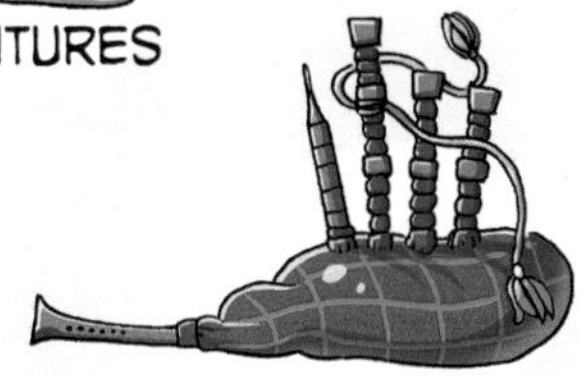

BAGPIPES

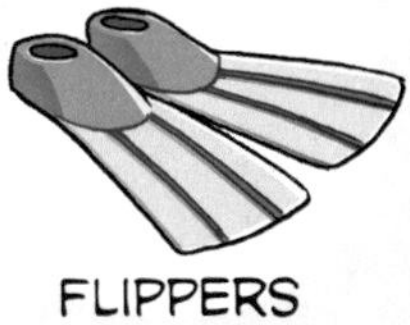

FLIPPERS

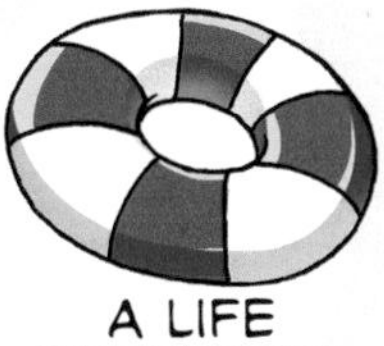

A LIFE PRESERVER

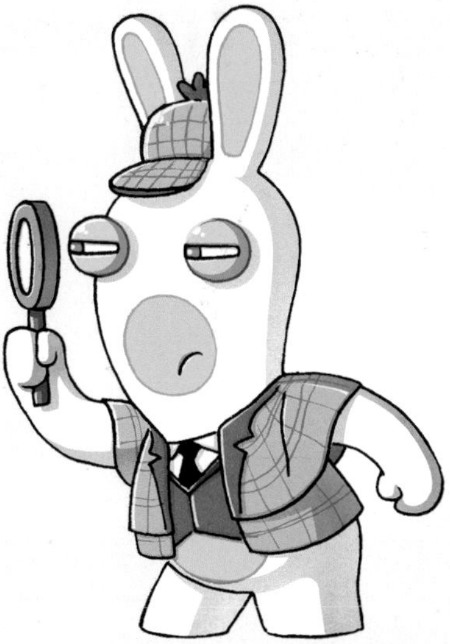

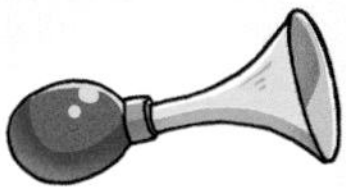

A HORN

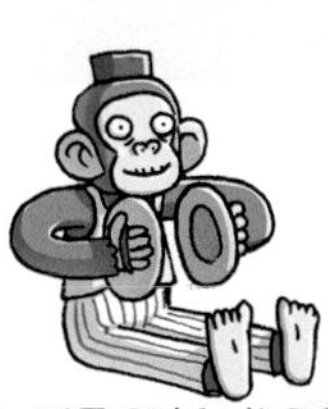

A MECHANICAL MONKEY

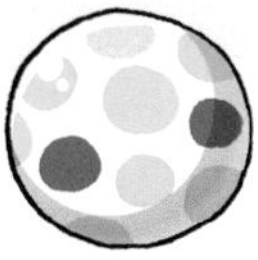

A BALL

WILL YOU BE ABLE TO SPOT THEM?

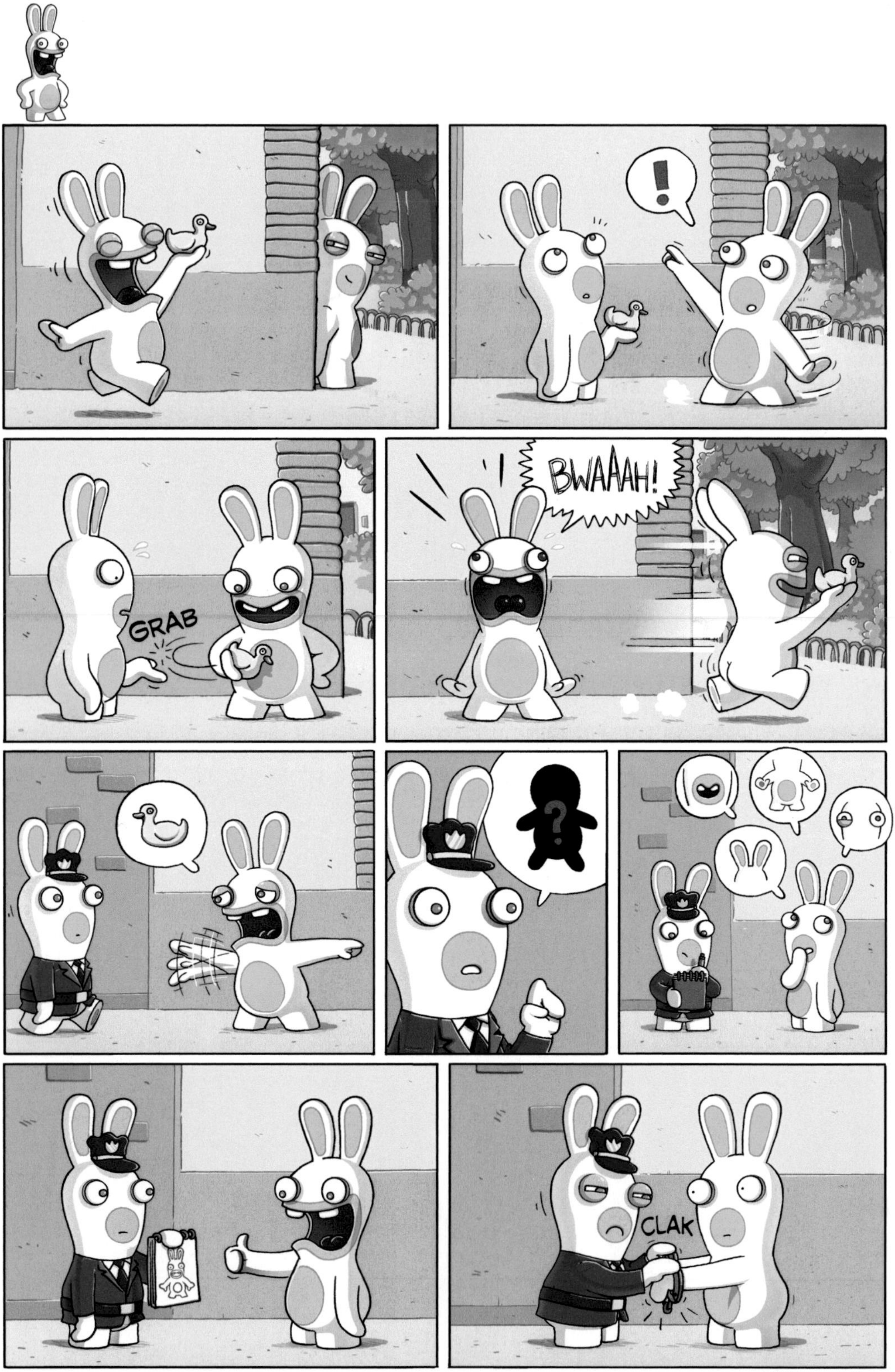
!
GRAB
BWAAAH!
CLAK

THITAUME -PUJOL-

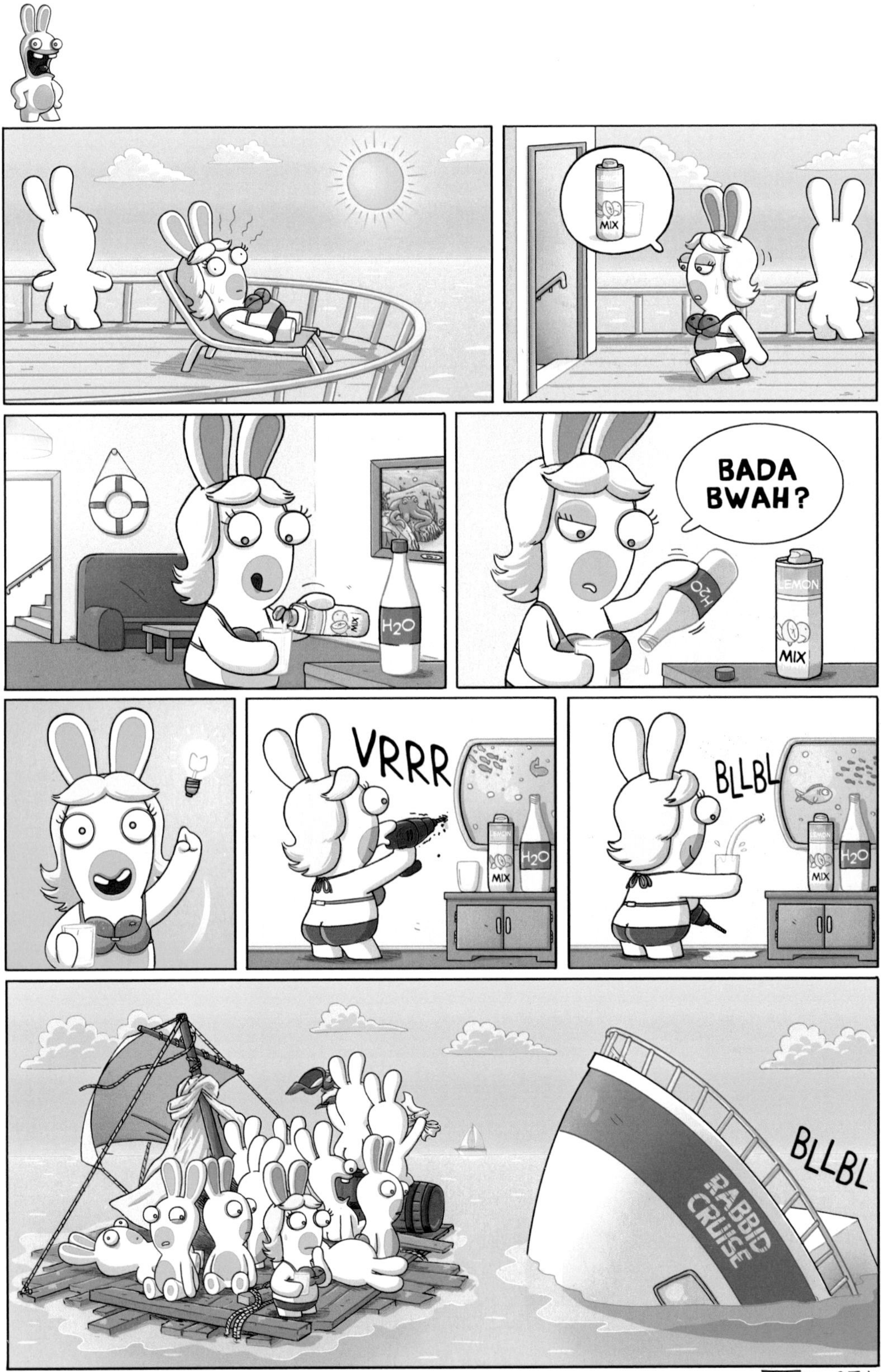
MIX
MIX
H2O
BADA BWAH?
LEMON
MIX
VRRR
BLLBL
RABBID CRUISE
BLLBL
THITAUME -PUJOL-

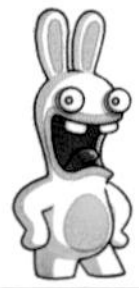

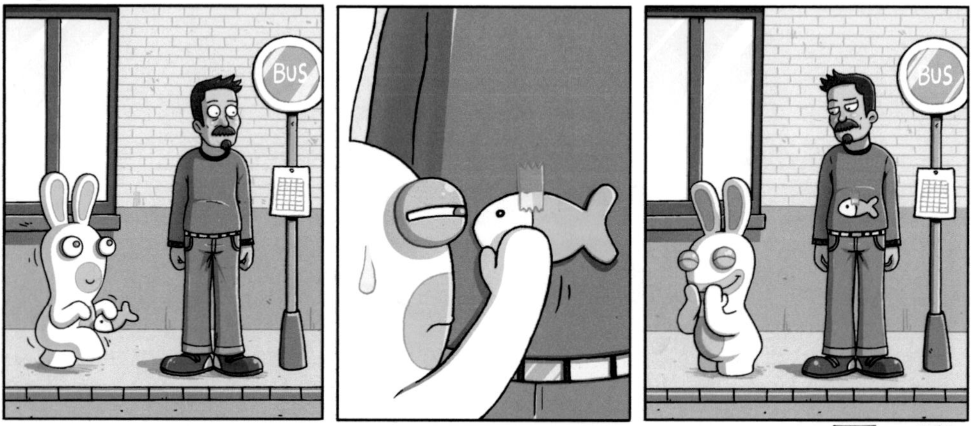
BUS
BUS

THITAUME -PUJOL-

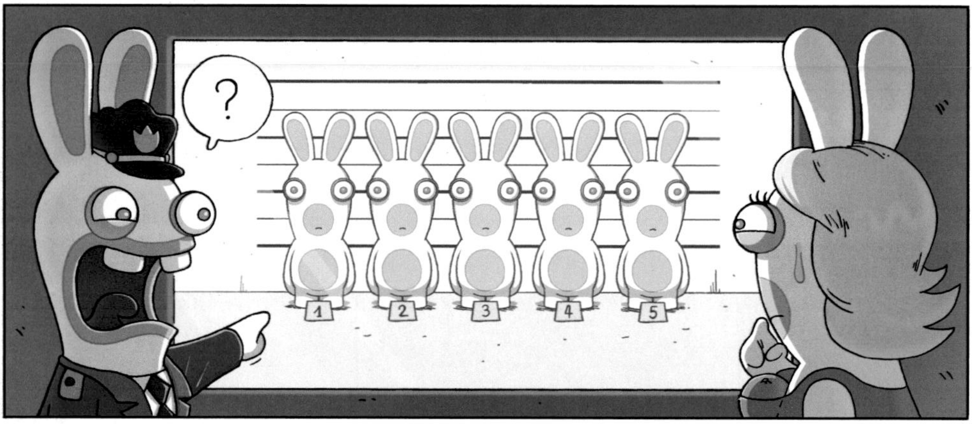
?
1
2
3
4
5

THITAUME -PUJOL-

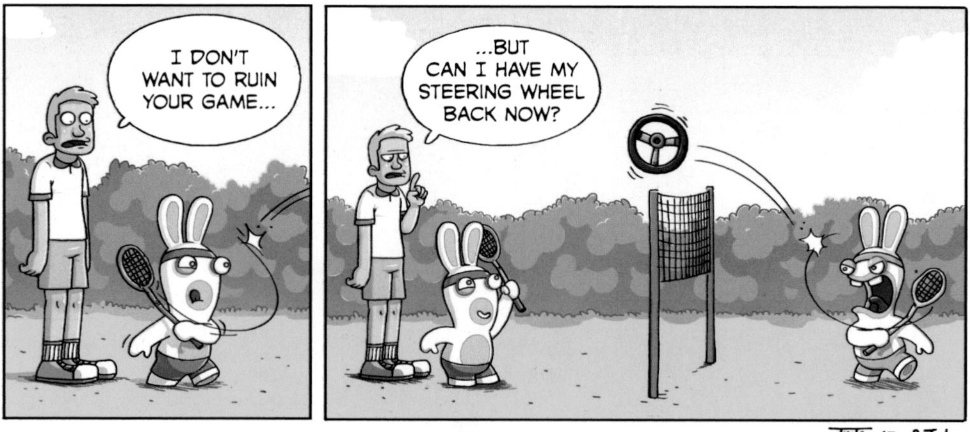
I DON'T WANT TO RUIN YOUR GAME...
...BUT CAN I HAVE MY STEERING WHEEL BACK NOW?

THITAUME -PUJOL-

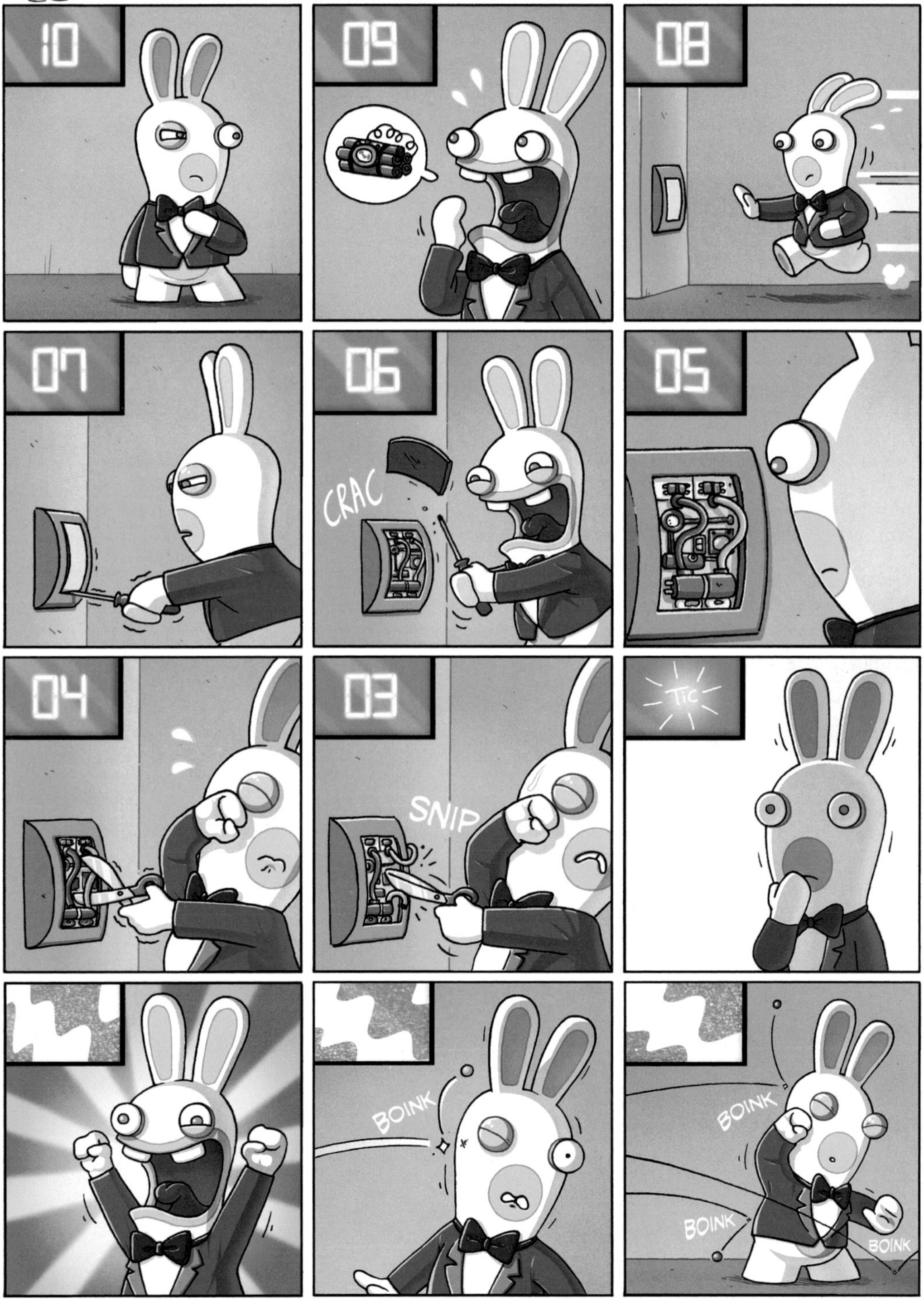
10
09
08
07
06
CRAC
05
04
03
SNIP
Tic
BOINK
BOINK
BOINK
BOINK

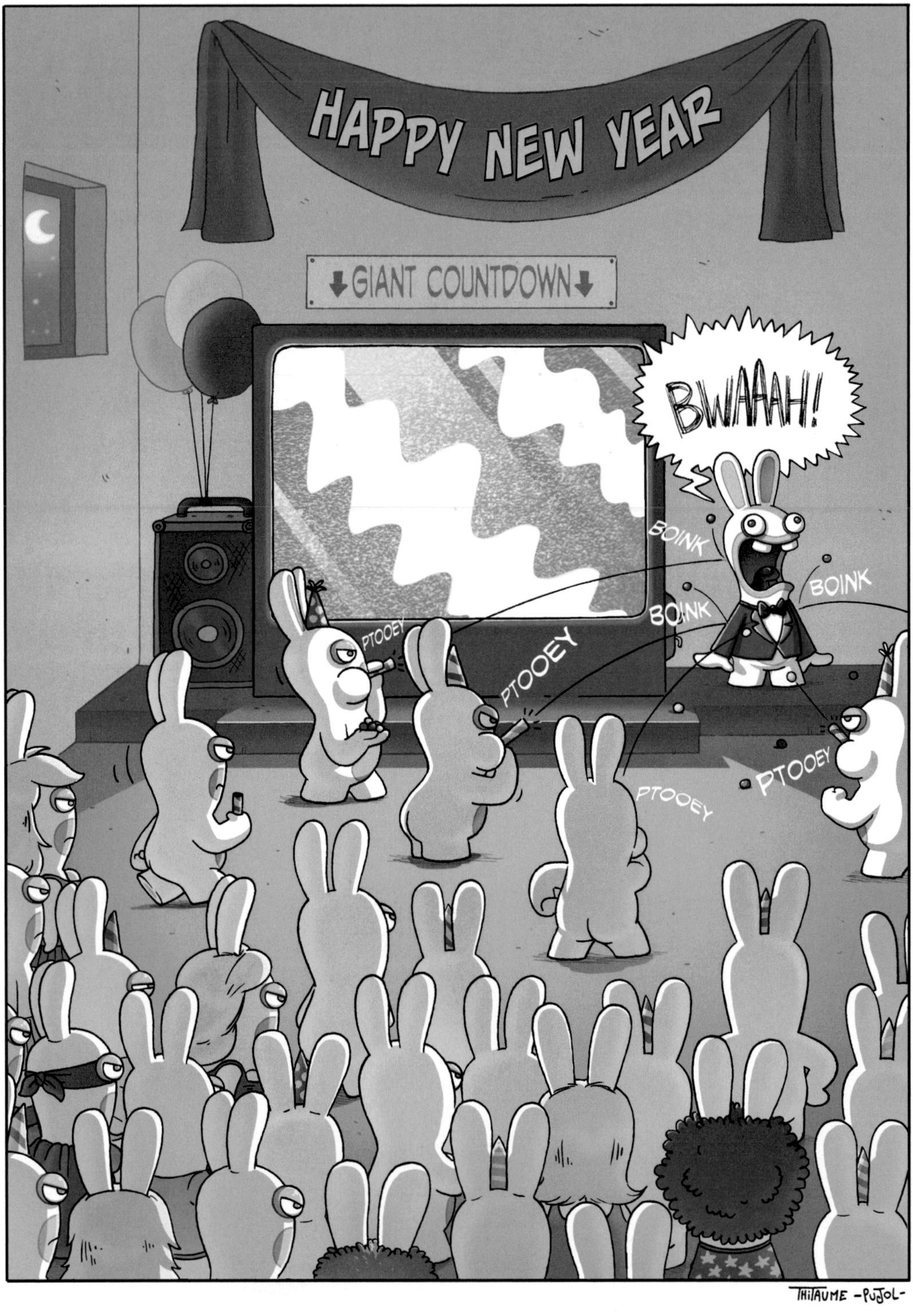
HAPPY NEW YEAR
GIANT COUNTDOWN
BWAAAH!
BOINK
BOINK
BOINK
PTOOEY
PTOOEY
PTOOEY
PTOOEY
PTOOEY
THITAUME -PUJOL-

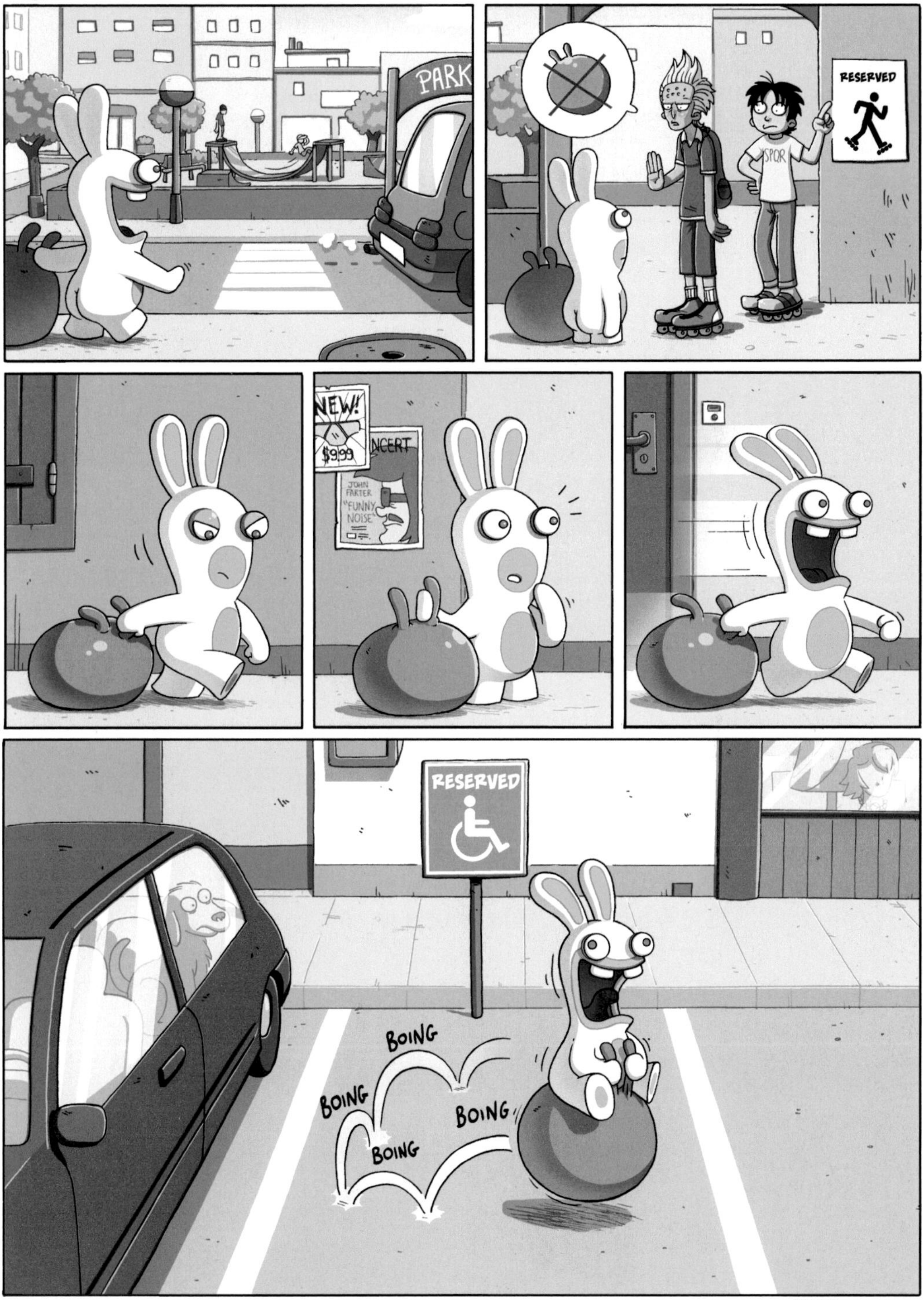
PARK
SPQR
RESERVED
NEW!
$9.99
NCERT
JOHN FARTER
"FUNNY NOISE"
RESERVED
BOING
BOING
BOING
BOING

THITAUME -PUJOL-

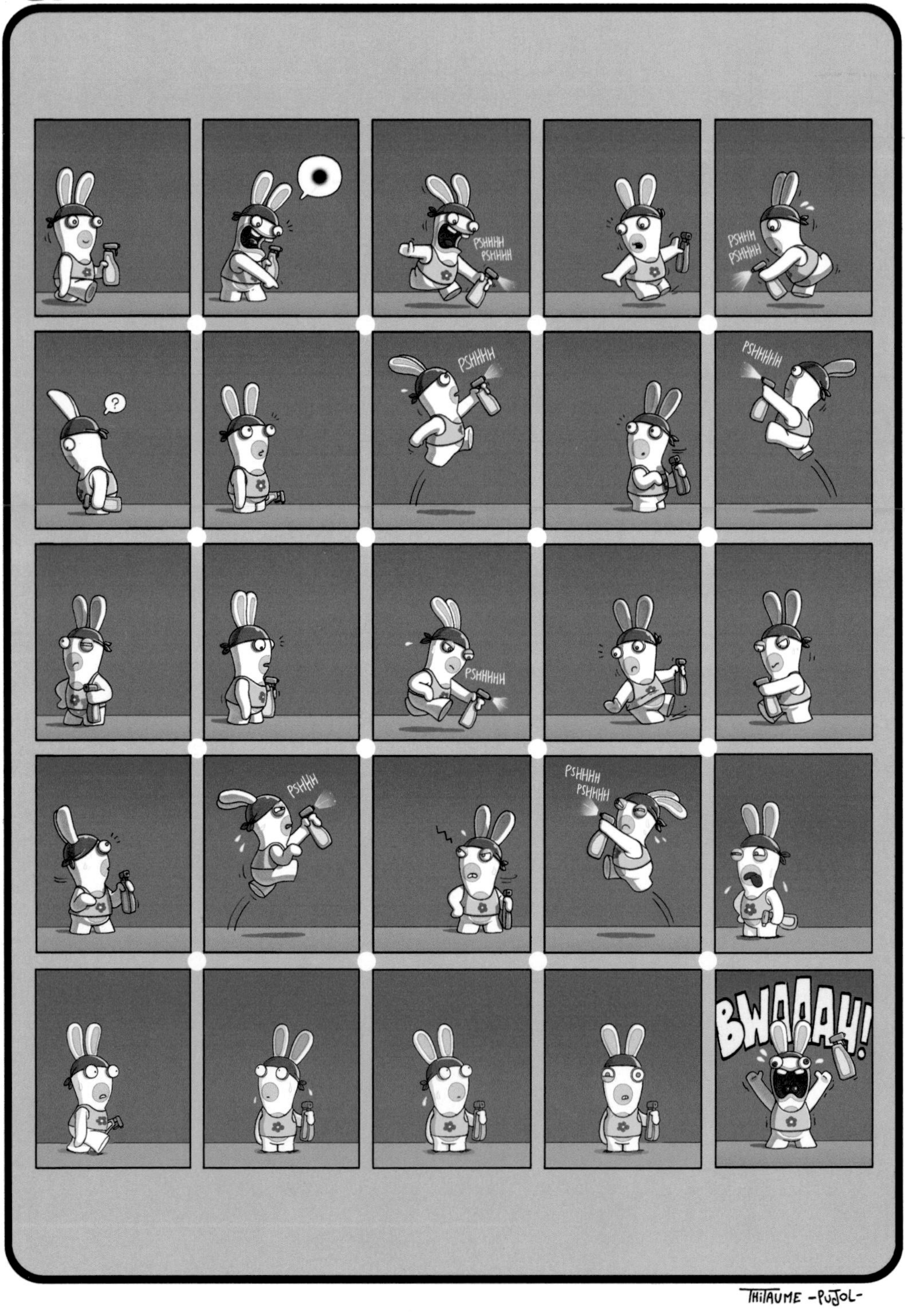

PSHHHH
PSHHHH
PSHHH
PSHHHH
?
PSHHHH
PSHHHHH
PSHHHHH
PSHHH
PSHHHH
PSHHHH
BWAAAH!
THITAUME -PUJOL-

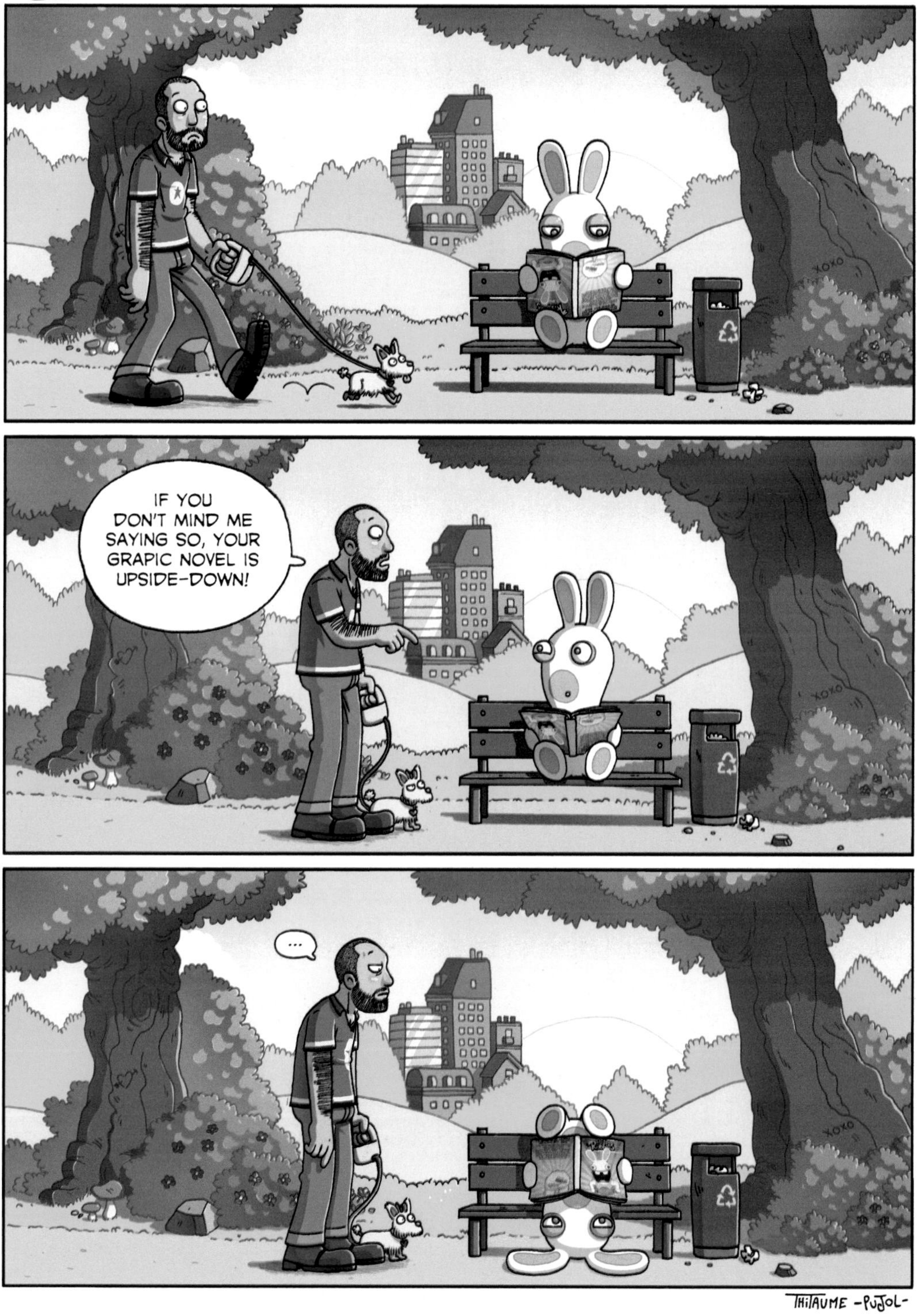
IF YOU DON'T MIND ME SAYING SO, YOUR GRAPIC NOVEL IS UPSIDE-DOWN!
...
THITAUME -PUJOL-

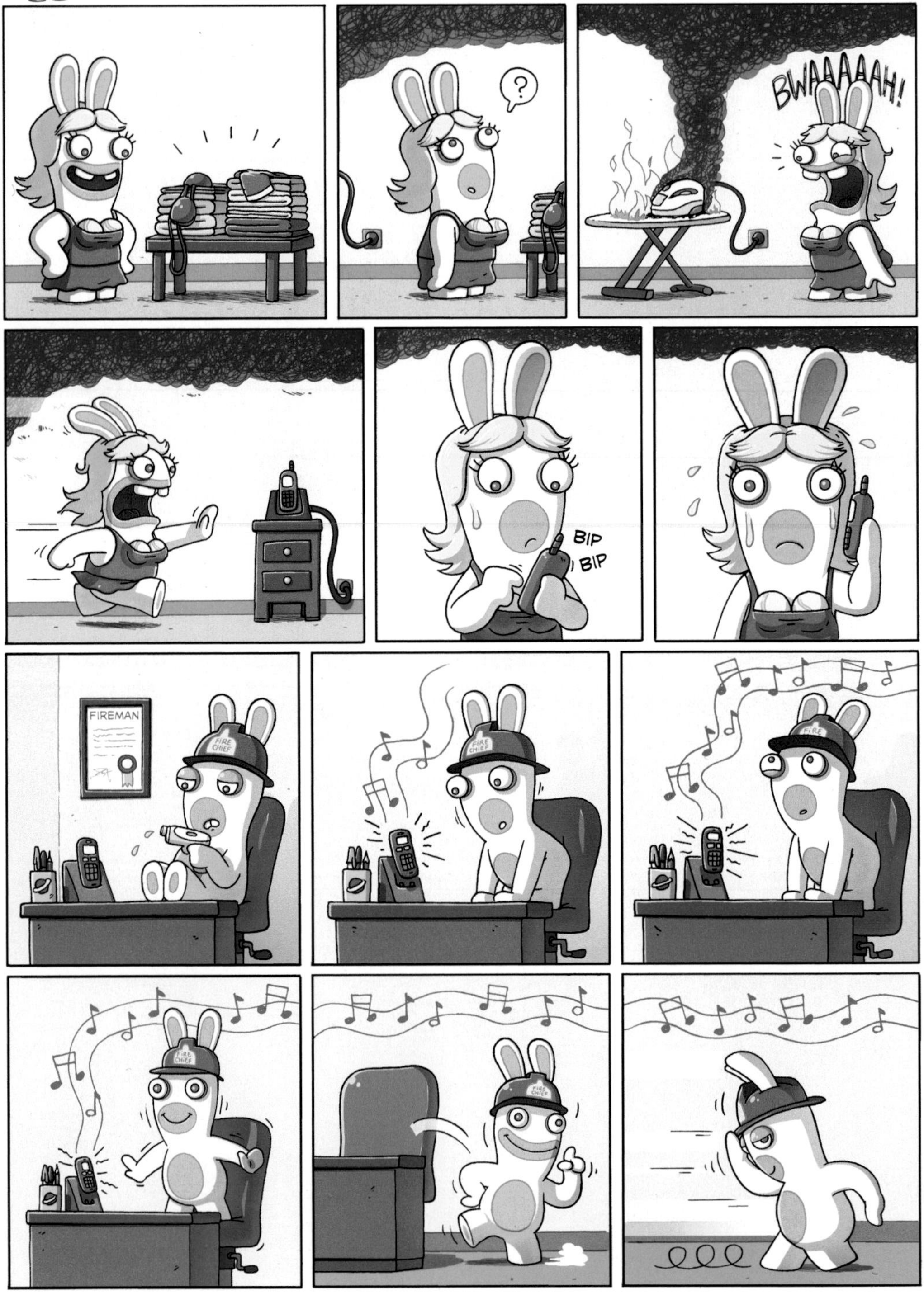
?
BWAAAAAH!
BIP
BIP
FIREMAN
FIRE CHIEF

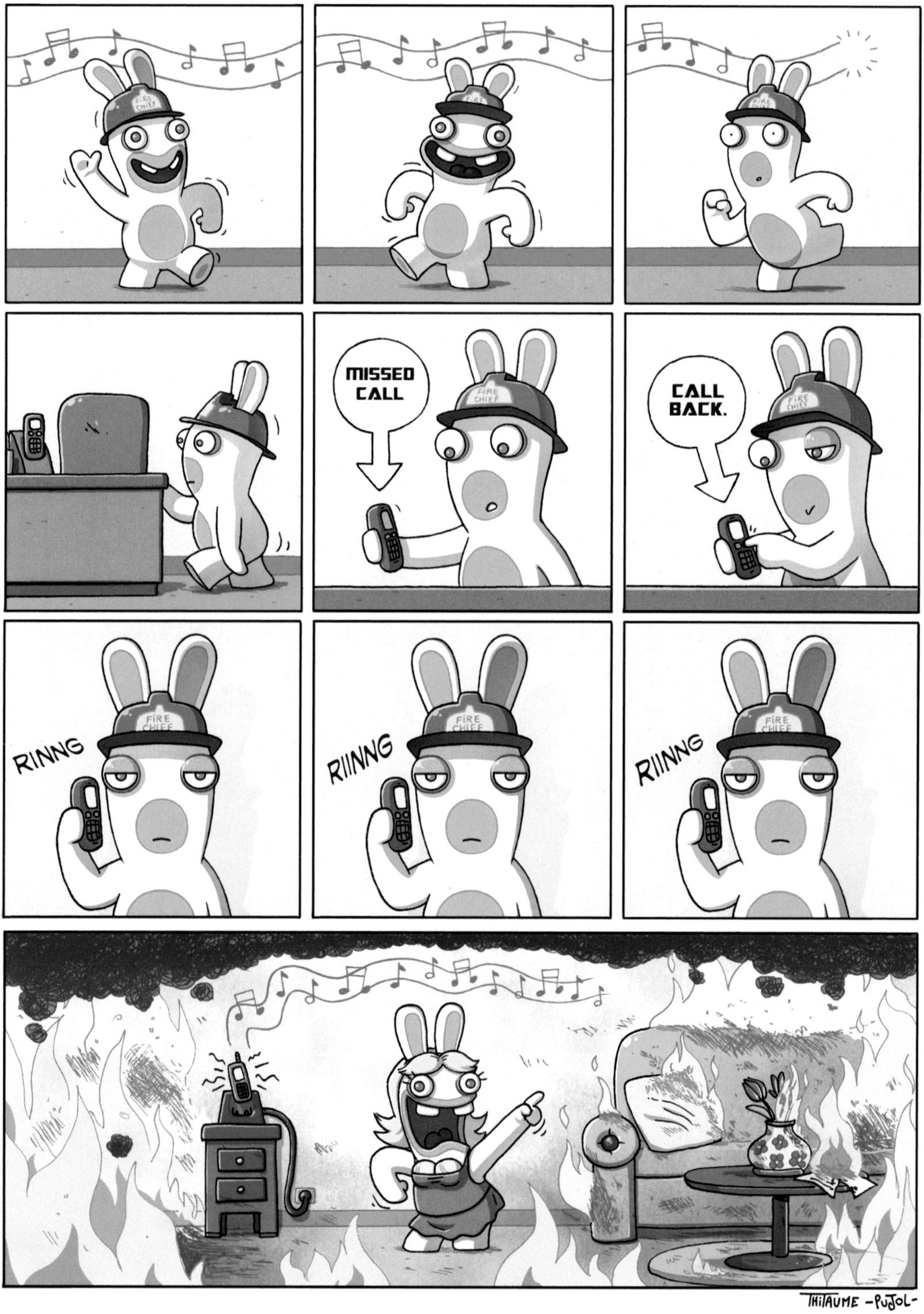
FIRE CHIEF
MISSED CALL
CALL BACK.
RINNG
RIINNG
RIINNG
THITAUME -PUJOL-

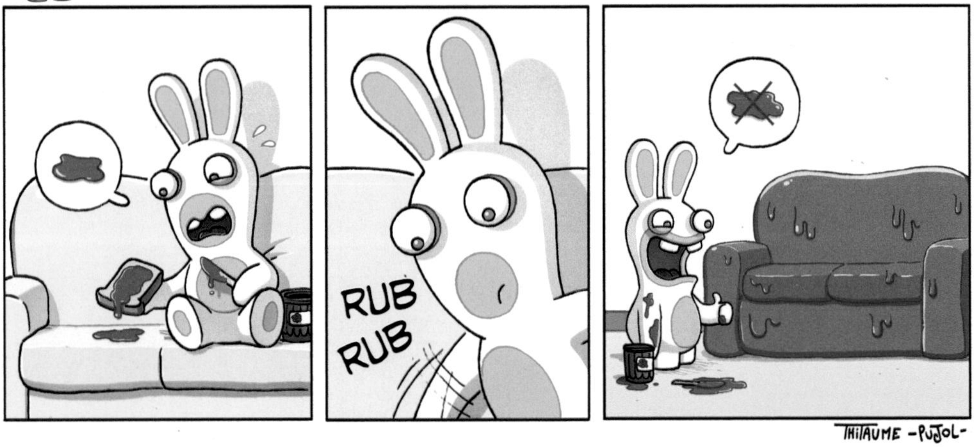
RUB
RUB
THITAUME -PUJOL-

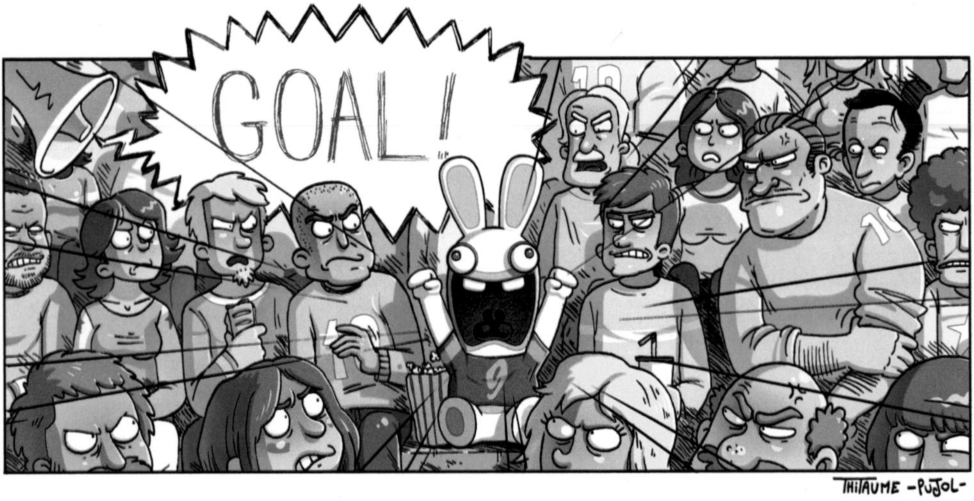
GOAL!
THITAUME -PUJOL-

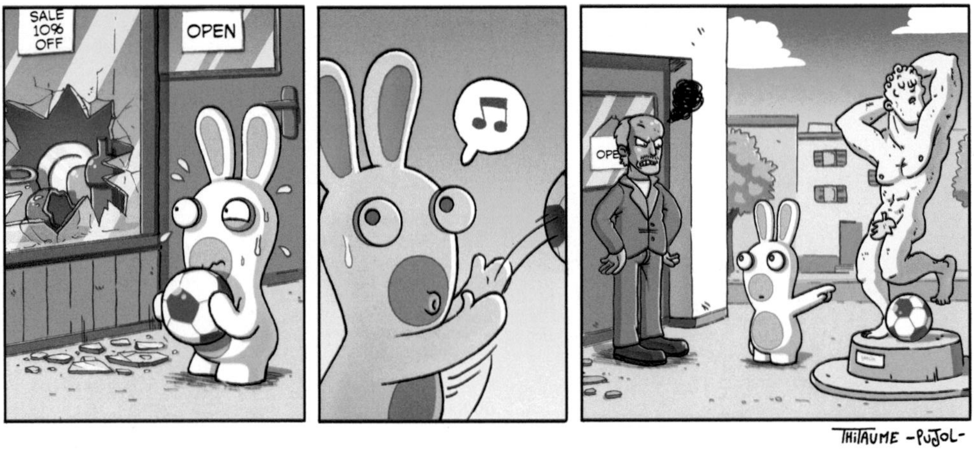
SALE
10% OFF
OPEN
THITAUME -PUJOL-

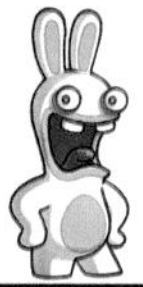

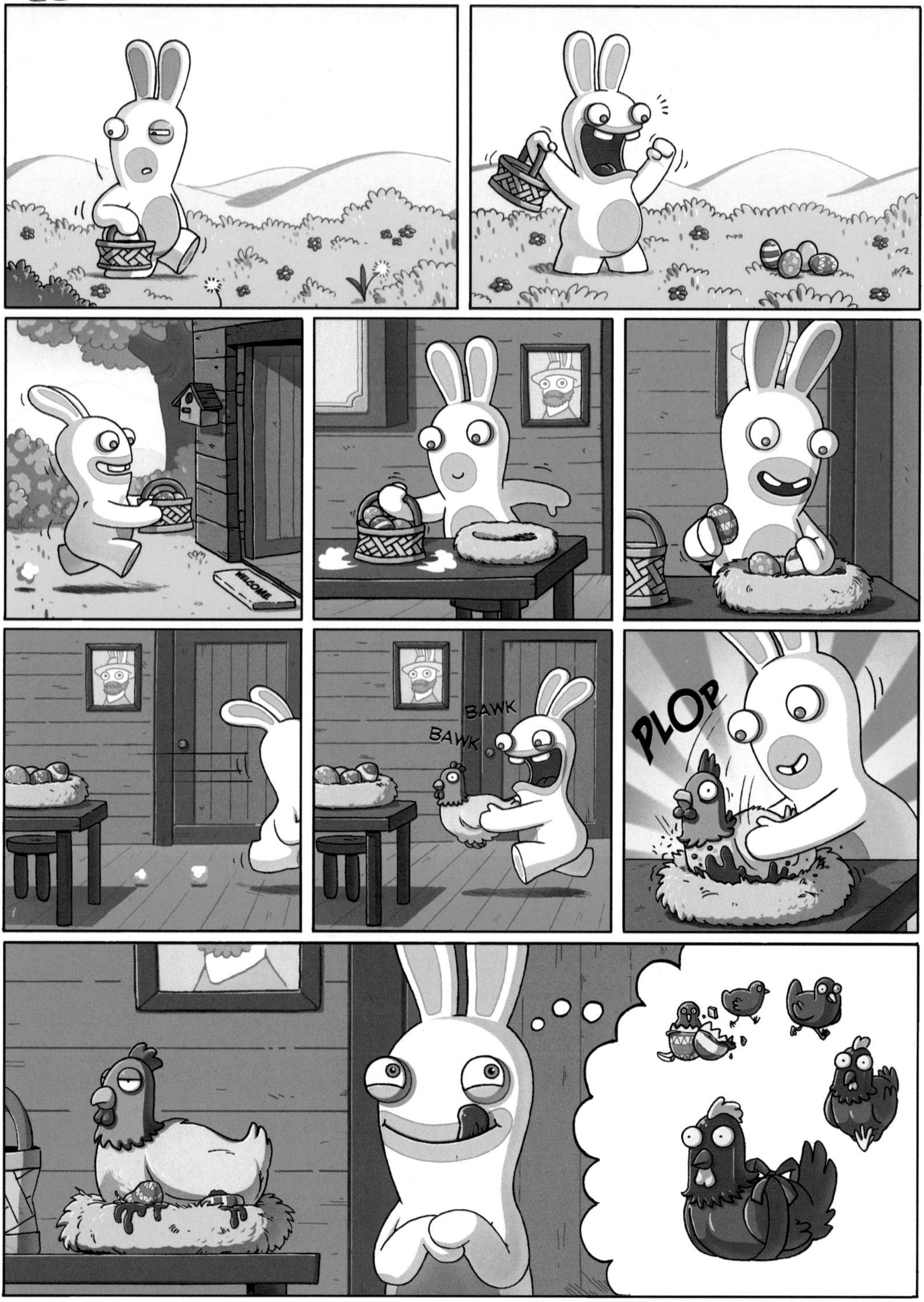
WELCOME
BAWK
BAWK
PLOP

THITAUME -PUJOL-

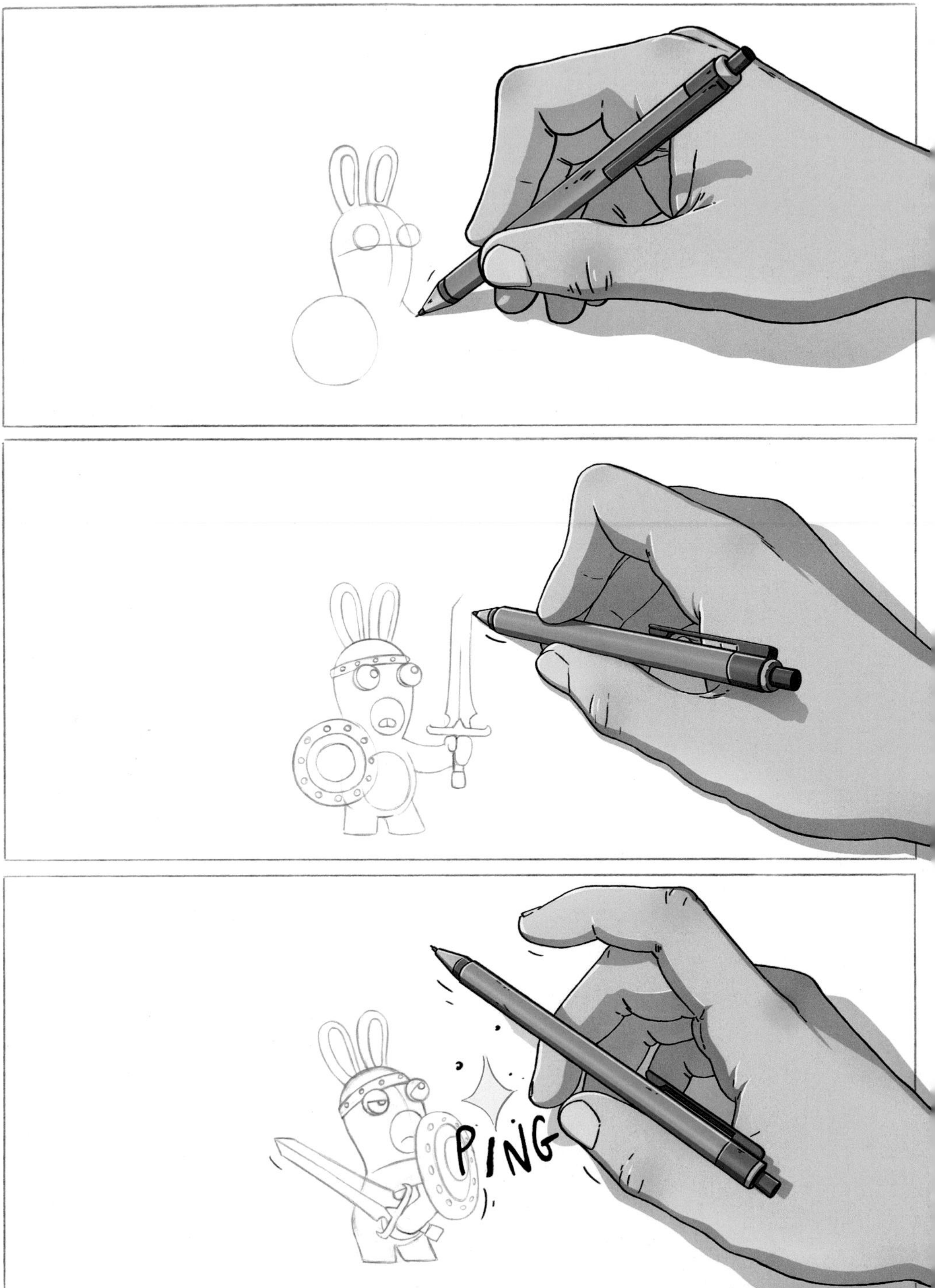
PING

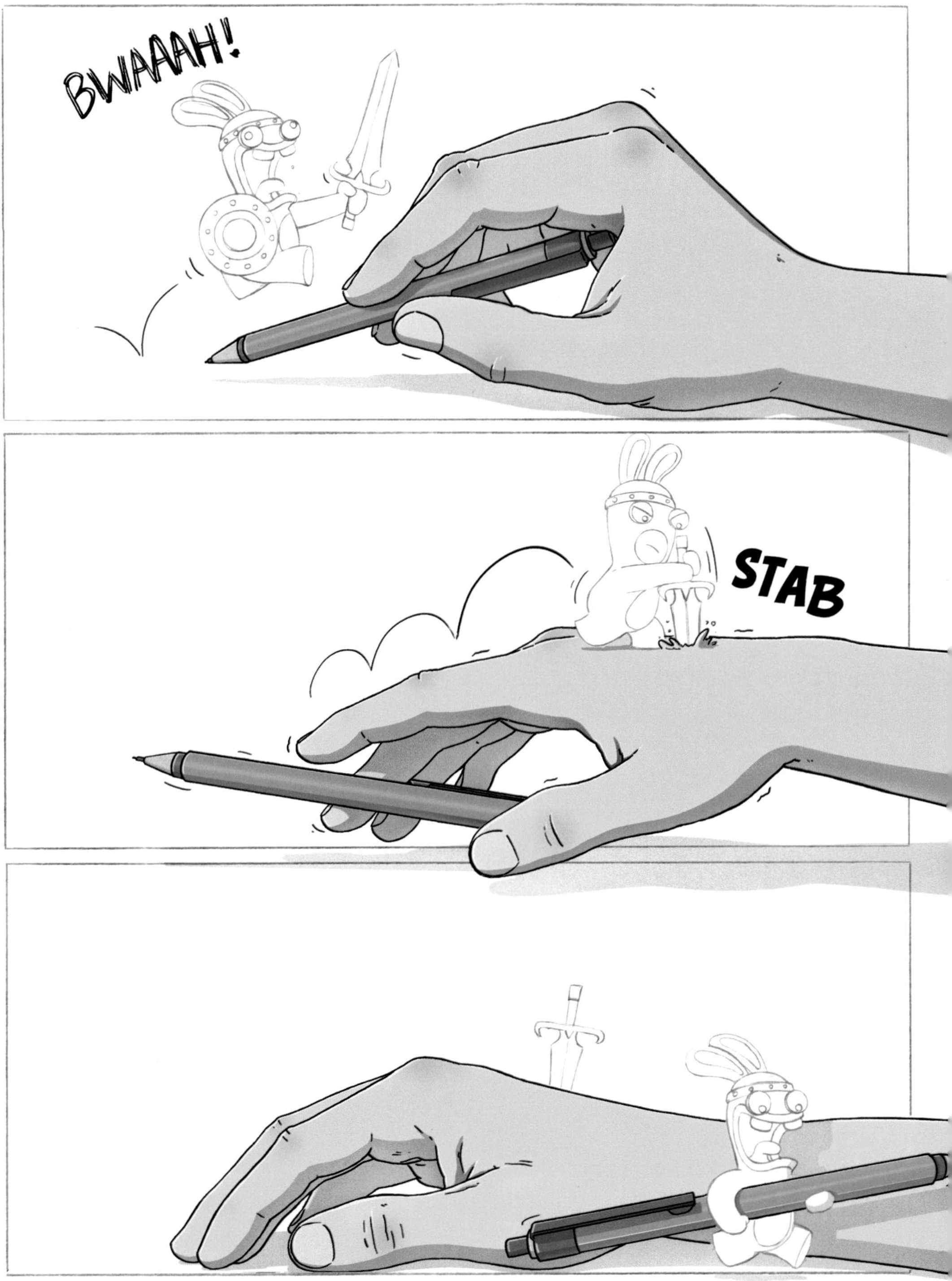
BWAAAH!
STAB

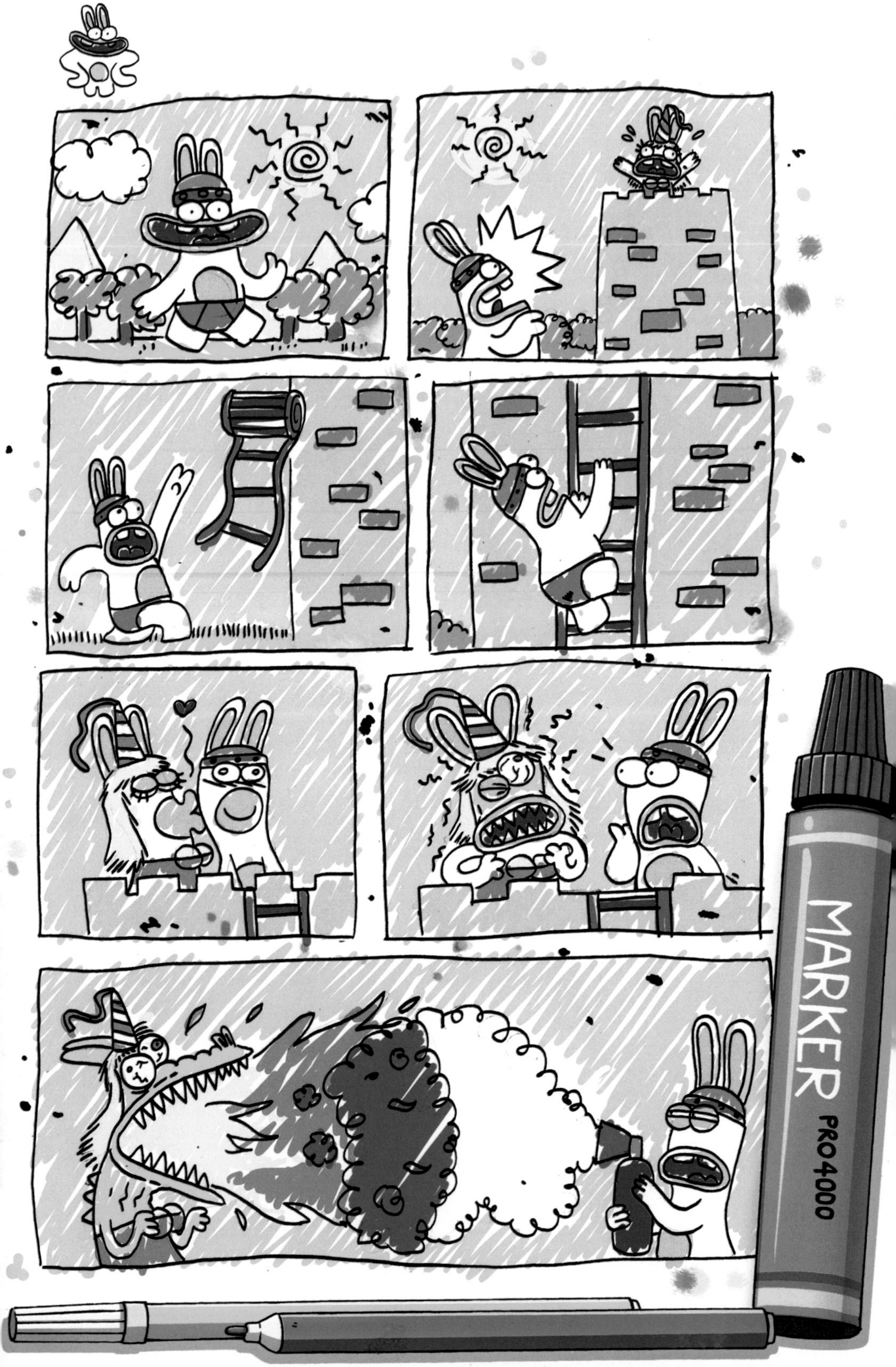
MARKER
PRO4000

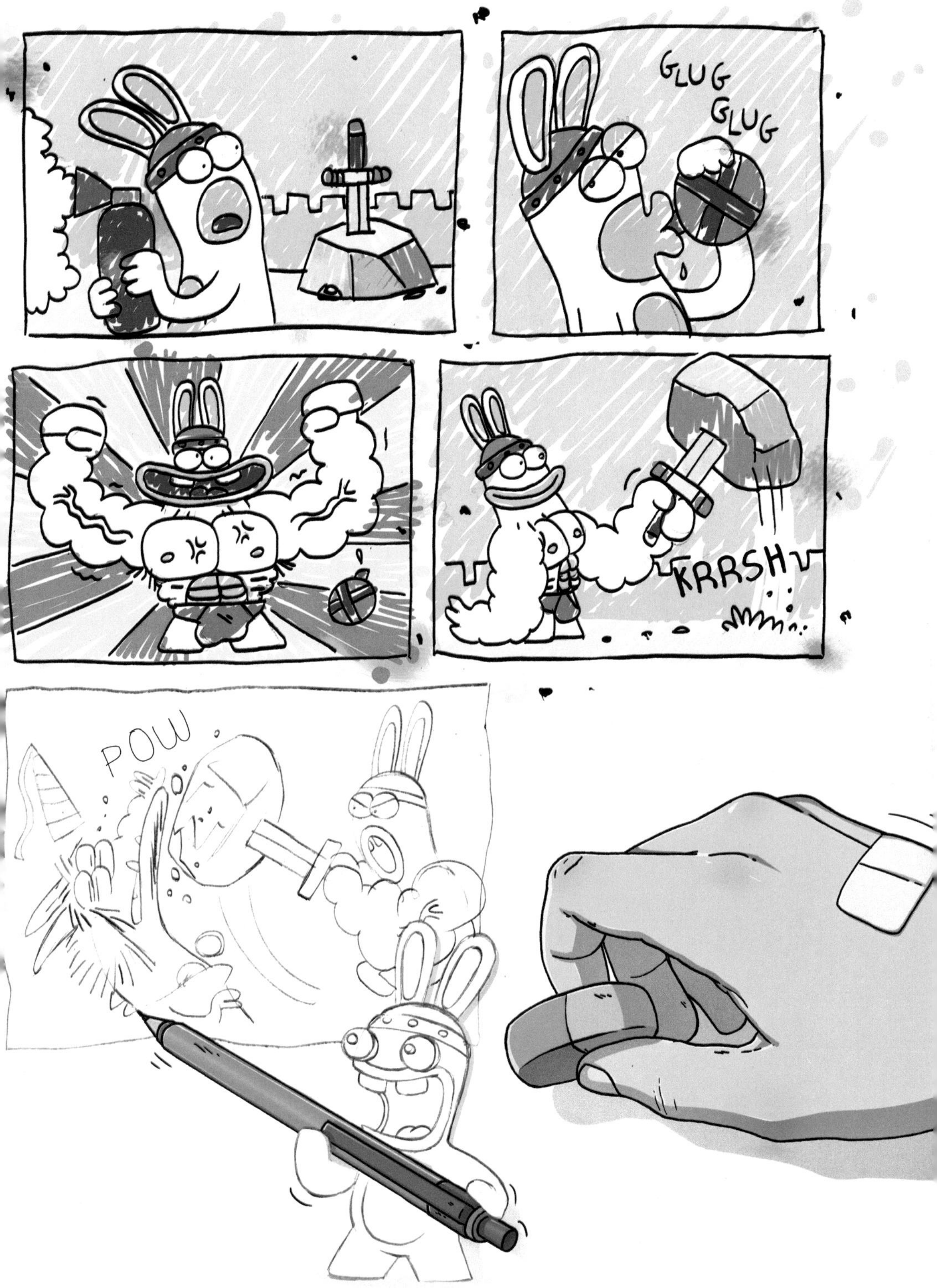
GLUG
GLUG
KRRSH
POW

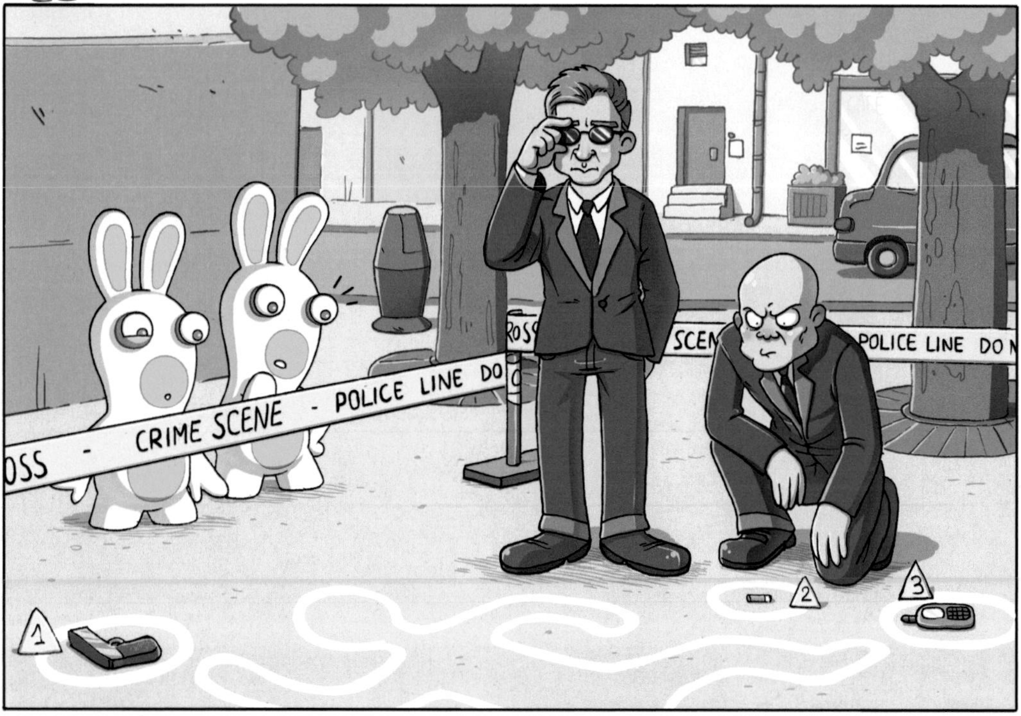
OSS - CRIME SCENE - POLICE LINE DO
ROSS
SCEN
POLICE LINE DO N

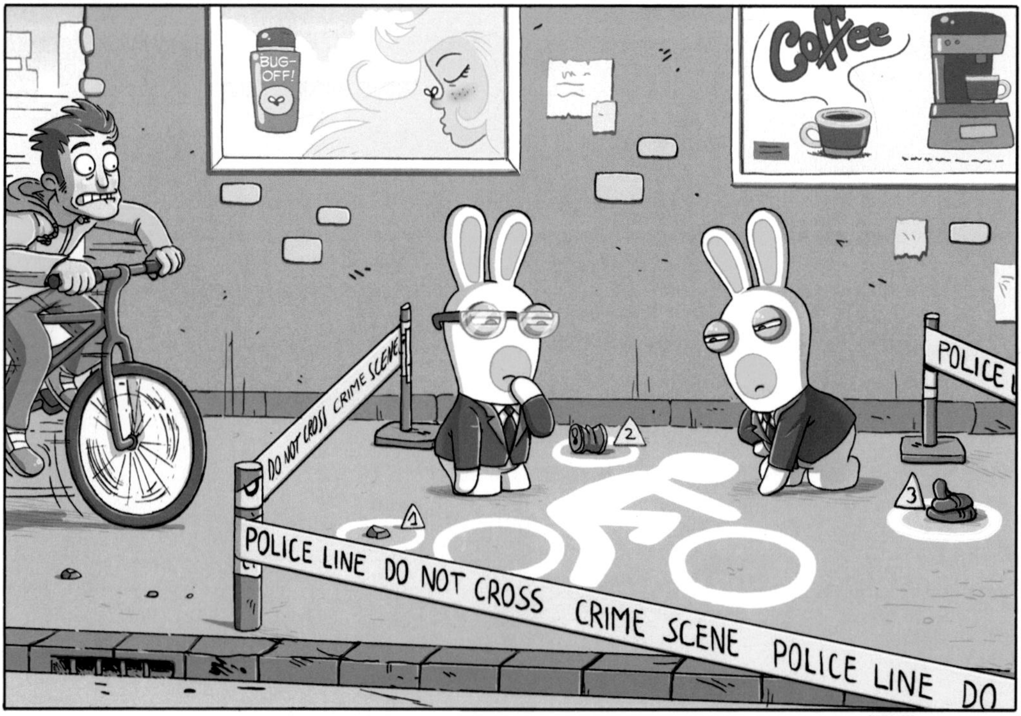
BUG-OFF!
Coffee
DO NOT CROSS CRIME SCENE
POLICE L
POLICE LINE DO NOT CROSS CRIME SCENE POLICE LINE DO

THITAUME -PUJOL-

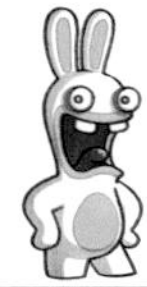

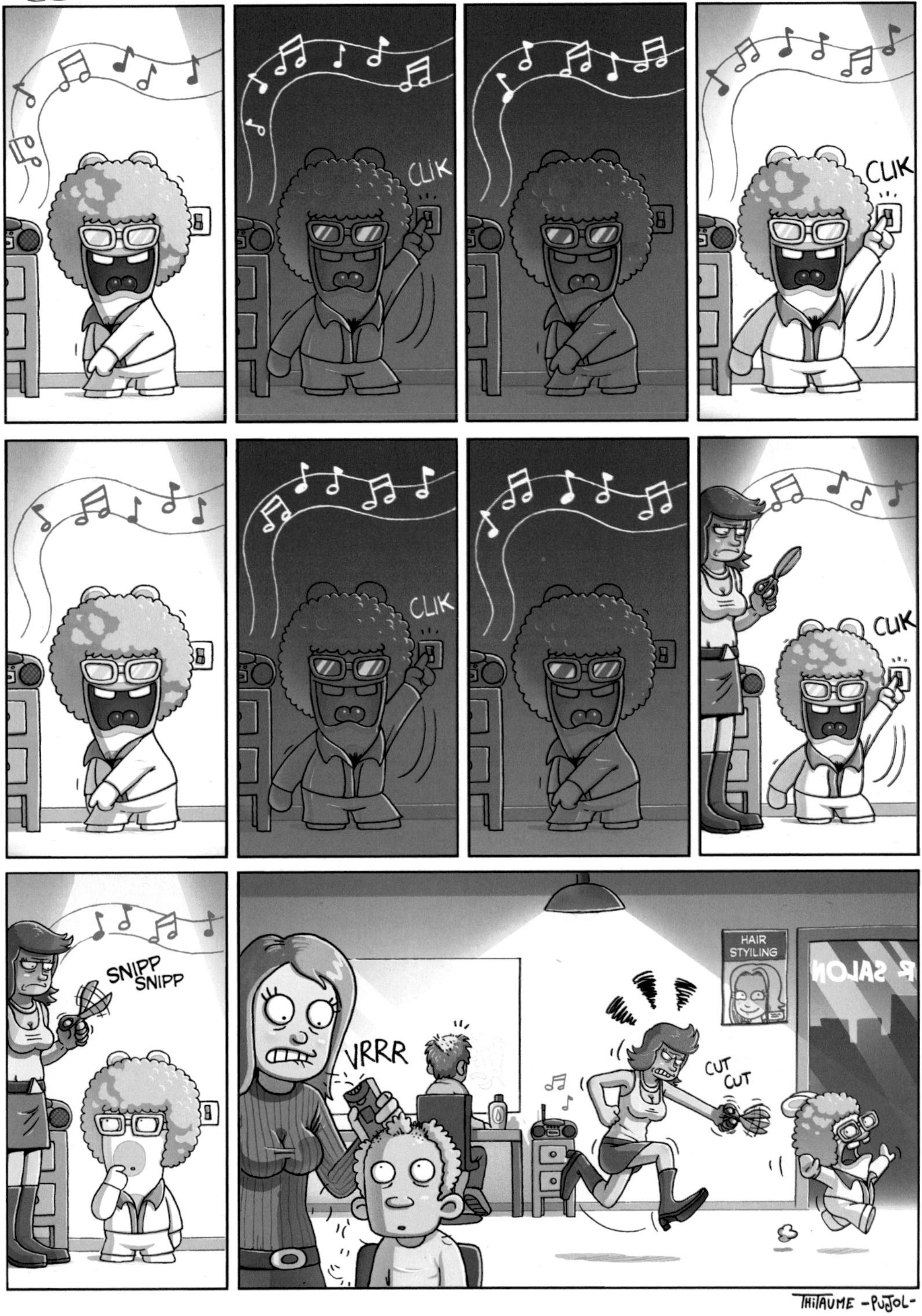

CLIK
CLIK
CLIK
CLIK
SNIPP
SNIPP
HAIR STYLING
VRRR
CUT
CUT
THITAUME -PUJOL-

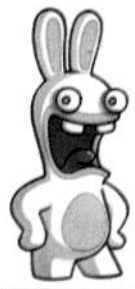

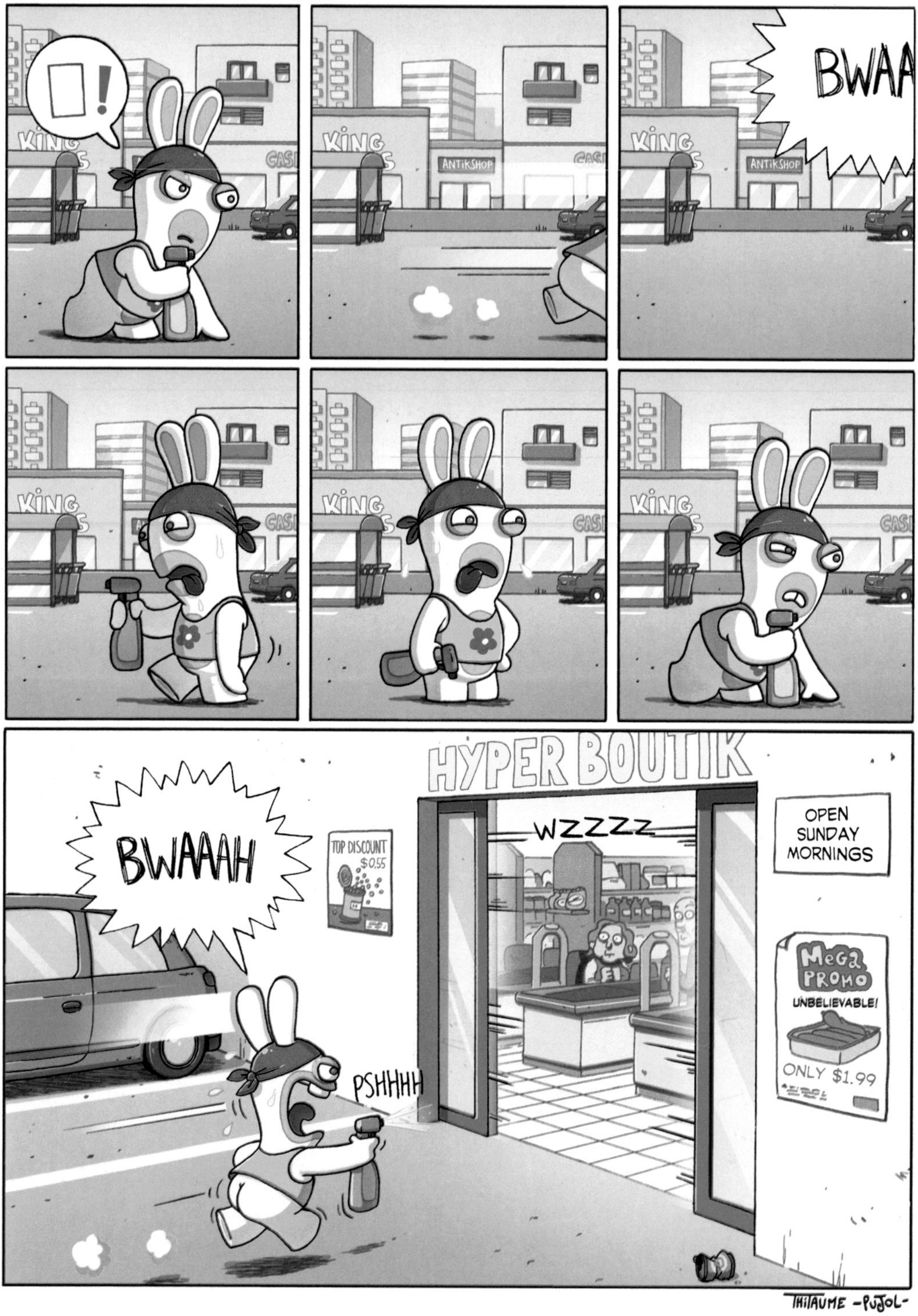
!
BWAA
ANTIKSHOP
HYPER BOUTIK
BWAAAH
TOP DISCOUNT
$0.55
WZZZZ
OPEN
SUNDAY
MORNINGS
Mega
PROMO
UNBELIEVABLE!
ONLY $1.99
PSHHHH
THITAUME -PUJOL-

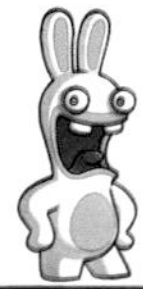

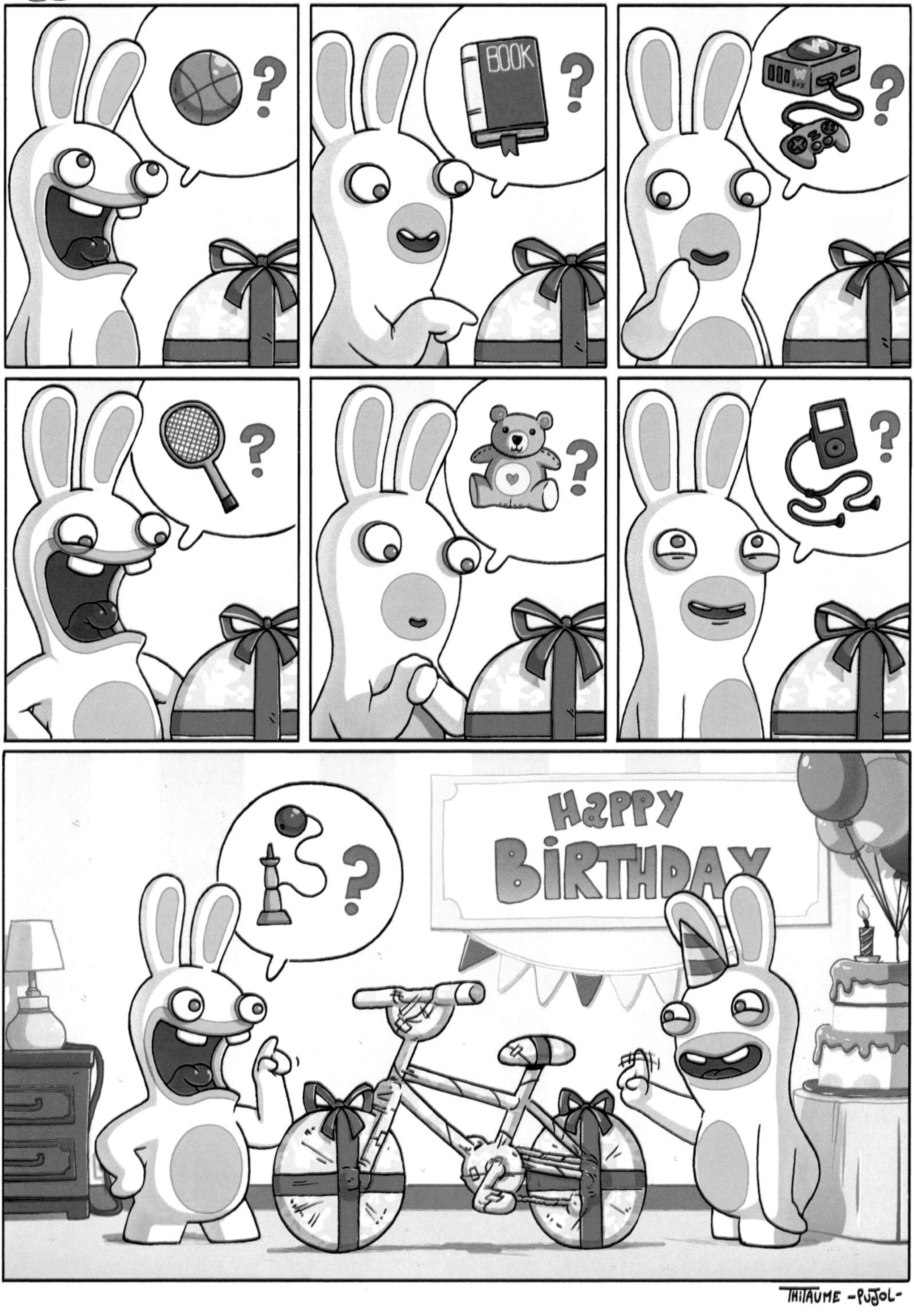
?
BOOK
?
?
?
?
?
?
HAPPY
BIRTHDAY

THITAUME -PUJOL-

AT THE PRINTER'S

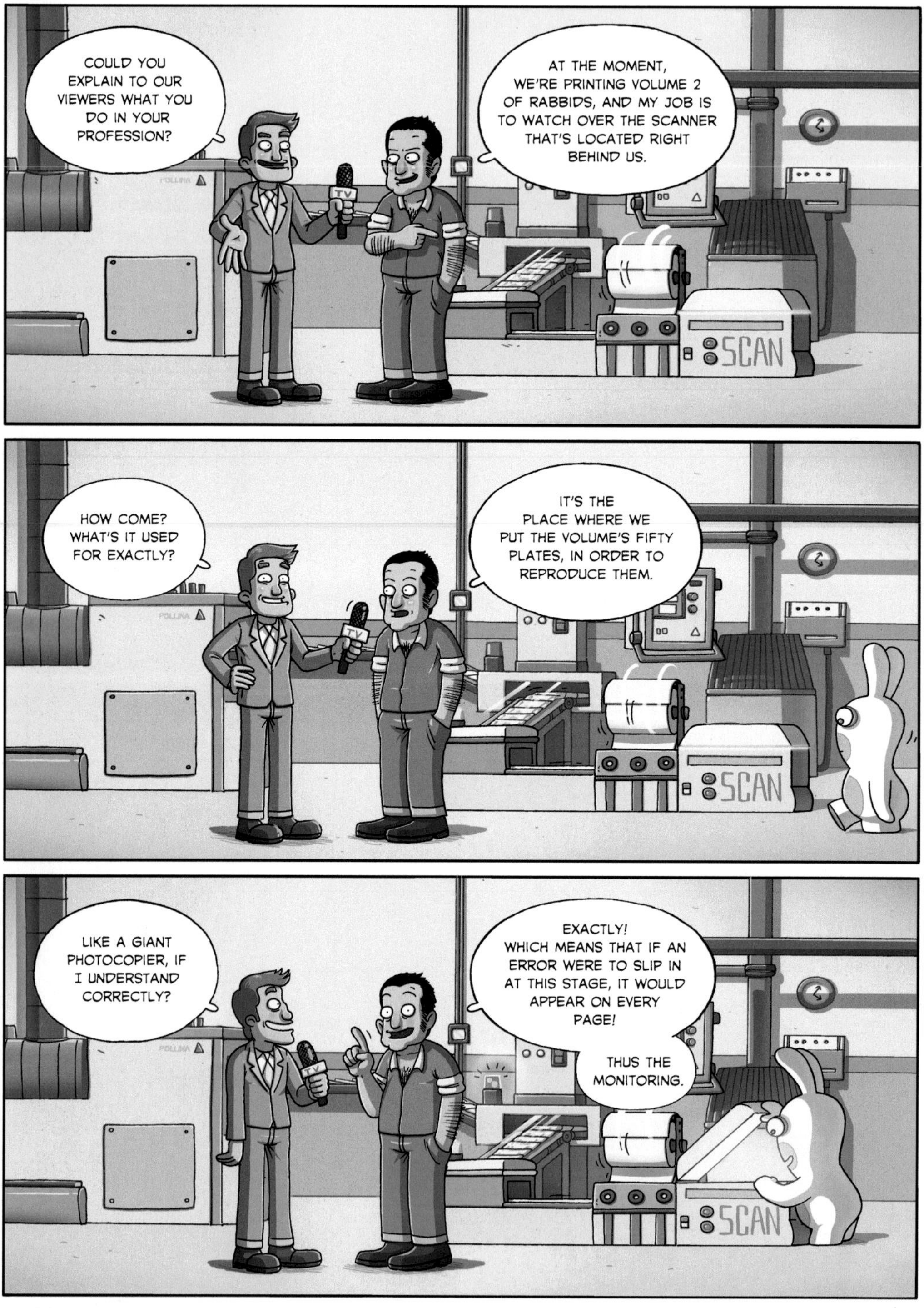
COULD YOU EXPLAIN TO OUR VIEWERS WHAT YOU DO IN YOUR PROFESSION?
AT THE MOMENT, WE'RE PRINTING VOLUME 2 OF RABBIDS, AND MY JOB IS TO WATCH OVER THE SCANNER THAT'S LOCATED RIGHT BEHIND US.
TV
SCAN
HOW COME? WHAT'S IT USED FOR EXACTLY?
IT'S THE PLACE WHERE WE PUT THE VOLUME'S FIFTY PLATES, IN ORDER TO REPRODUCE THEM.
TV
SCAN
LIKE A GIANT PHOTOCOPIER, IF I UNDERSTAND CORRECTLY?
EXACTLY! WHICH MEANS THAT IF AN ERROR WERE TO SLIP IN AT THIS STAGE, IT WOULD APPEAR ON EVERY PAGE!
THUS THE MONITORING.
TV
SCAN

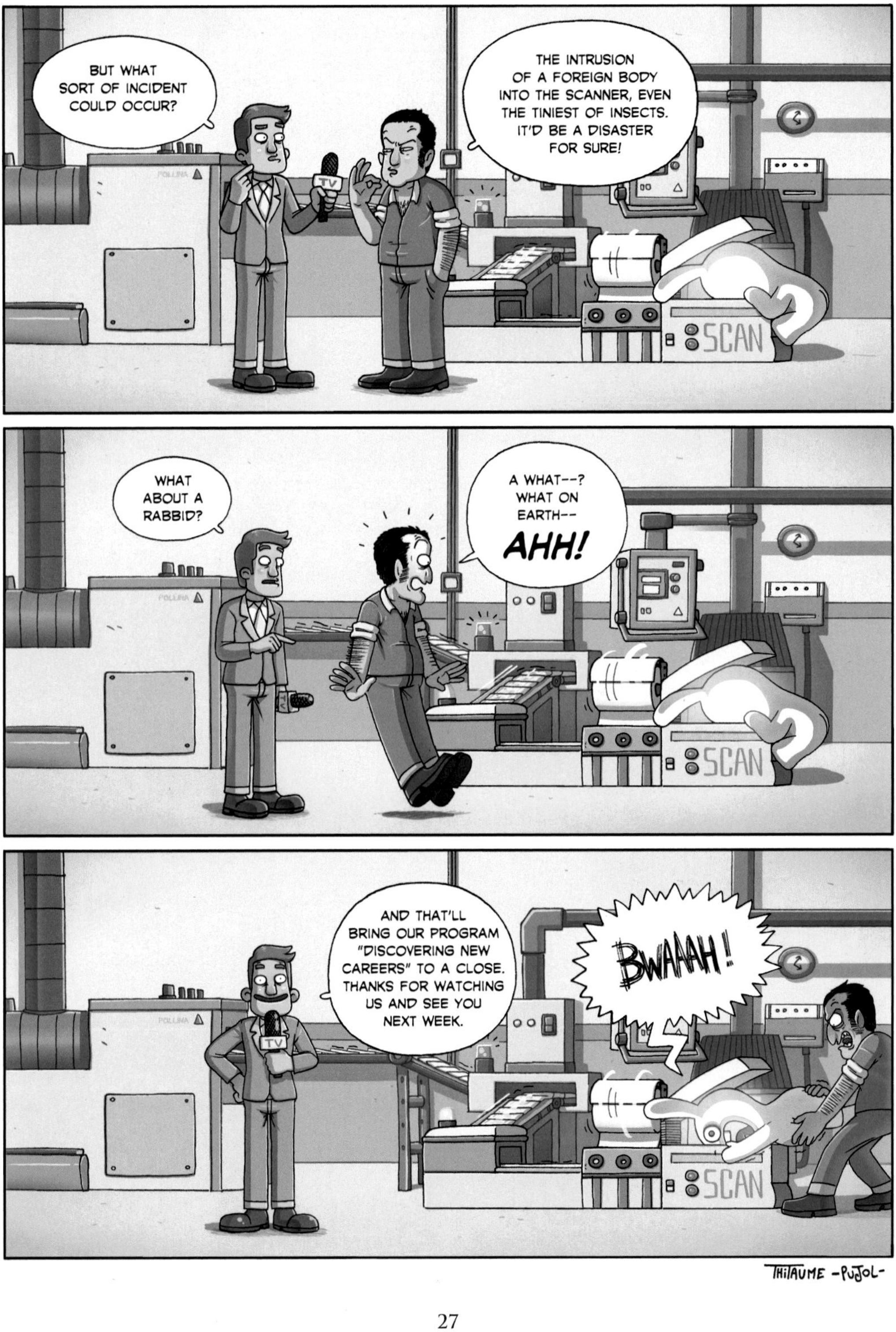
BUT WHAT SORT OF INCIDENT COULD OCCUR?
THE INTRUSION OF A FOREIGN BODY INTO THE SCANNER, EVEN THE TINIEST OF INSECTS. IT'D BE A DISASTER FOR SURE!
WHAT ABOUT A RABBID?
A WHAT--? WHAT ON EARTH--
AHH!
AND THAT'LL BRING OUR PROGRAM "DISCOVERING NEW CAREERS" TO A CLOSE. THANKS FOR WATCHING US AND SEE YOU NEXT WEEK.
BWAAAH!
SCAN

THITAUME -PUJOL-

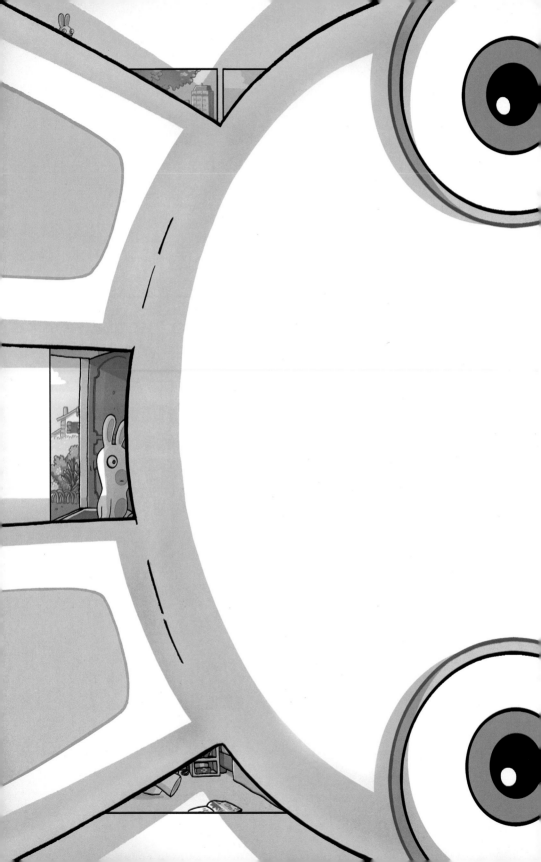

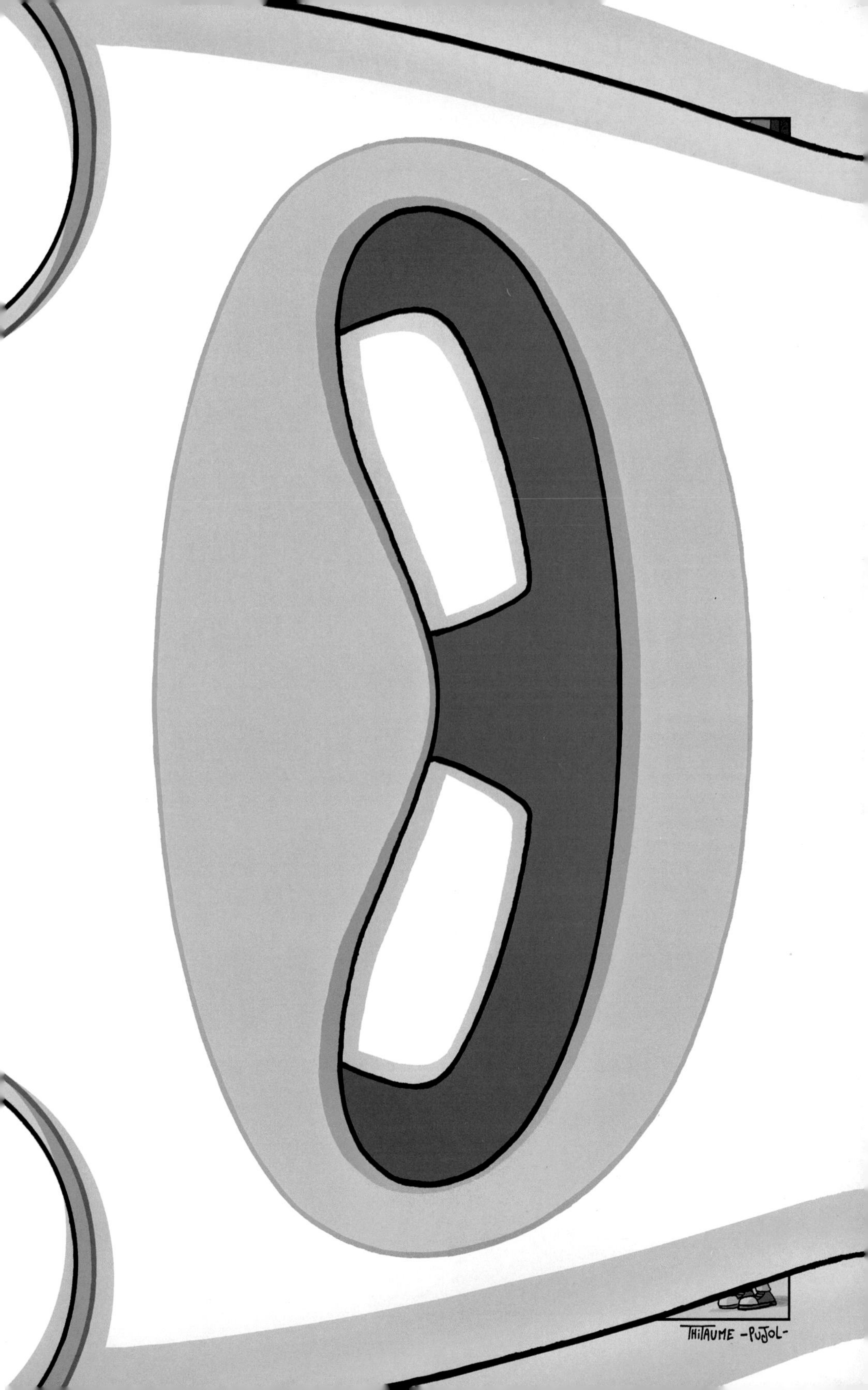
THITAUME -PUJOL-

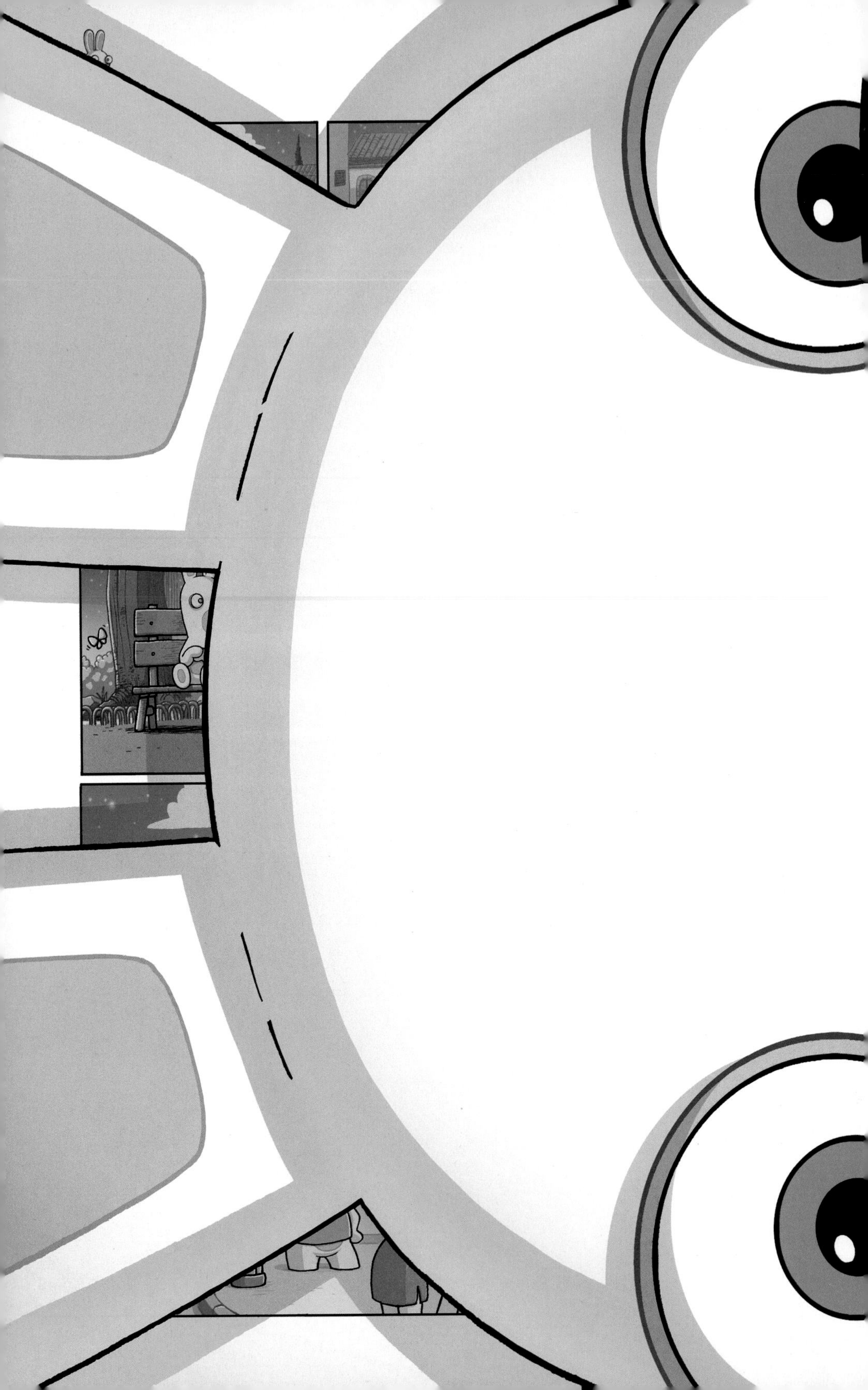

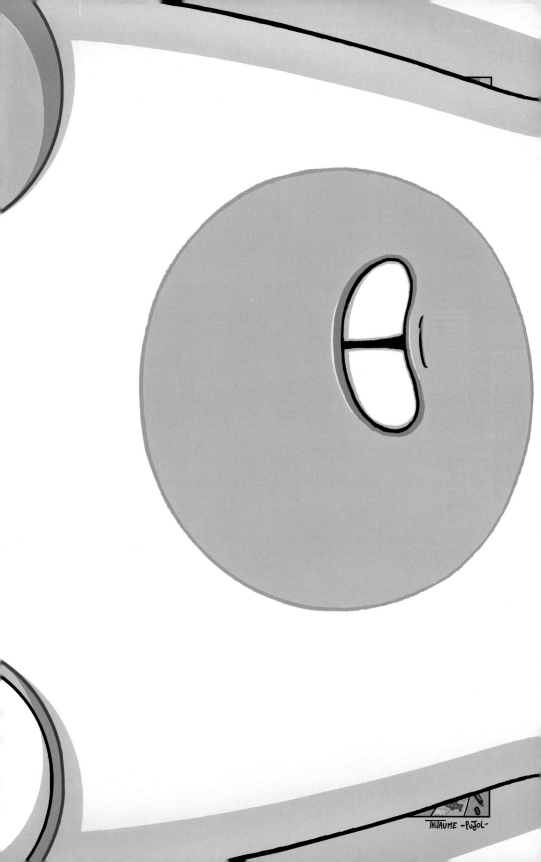

THIIAUME -PUJOL-

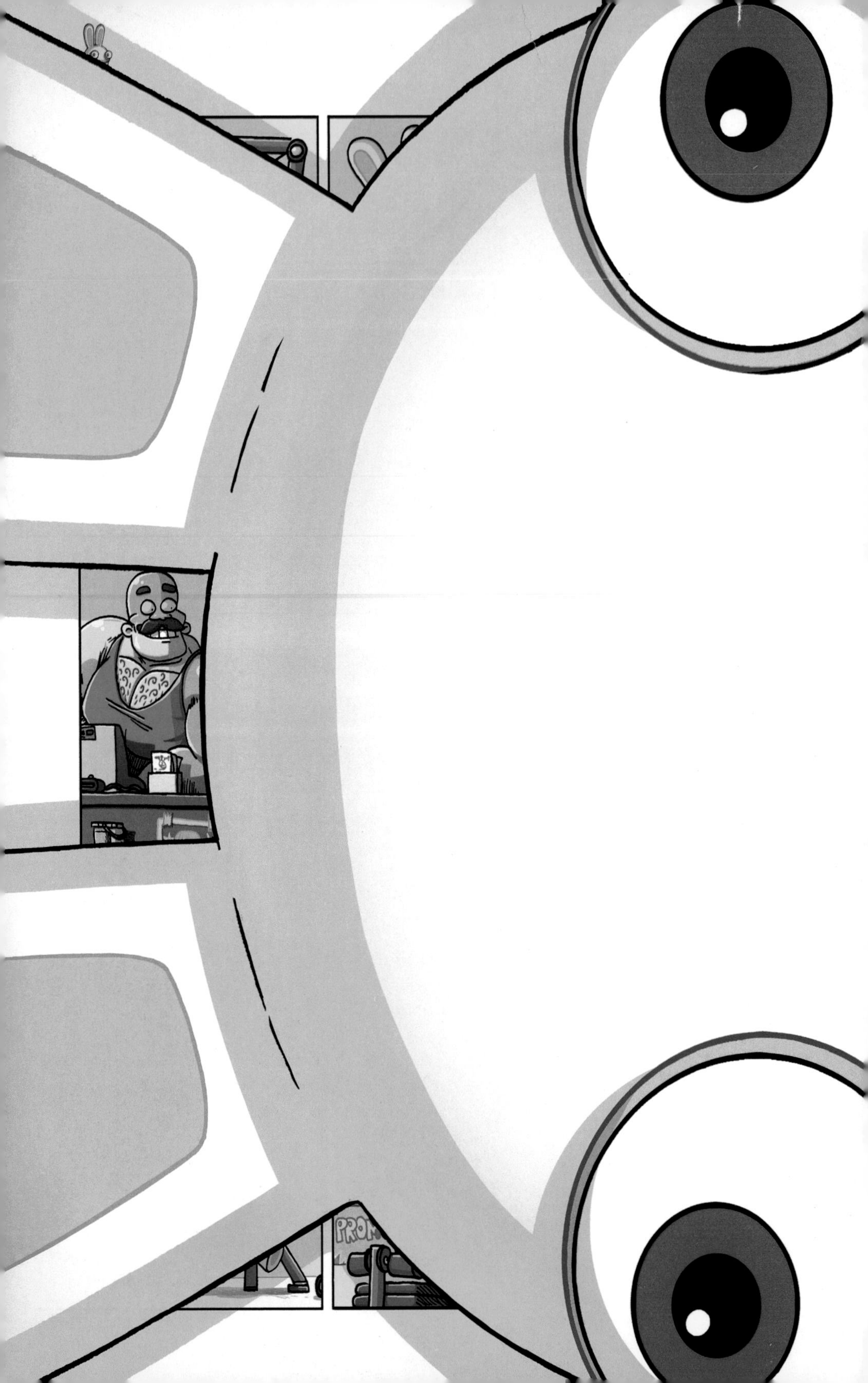

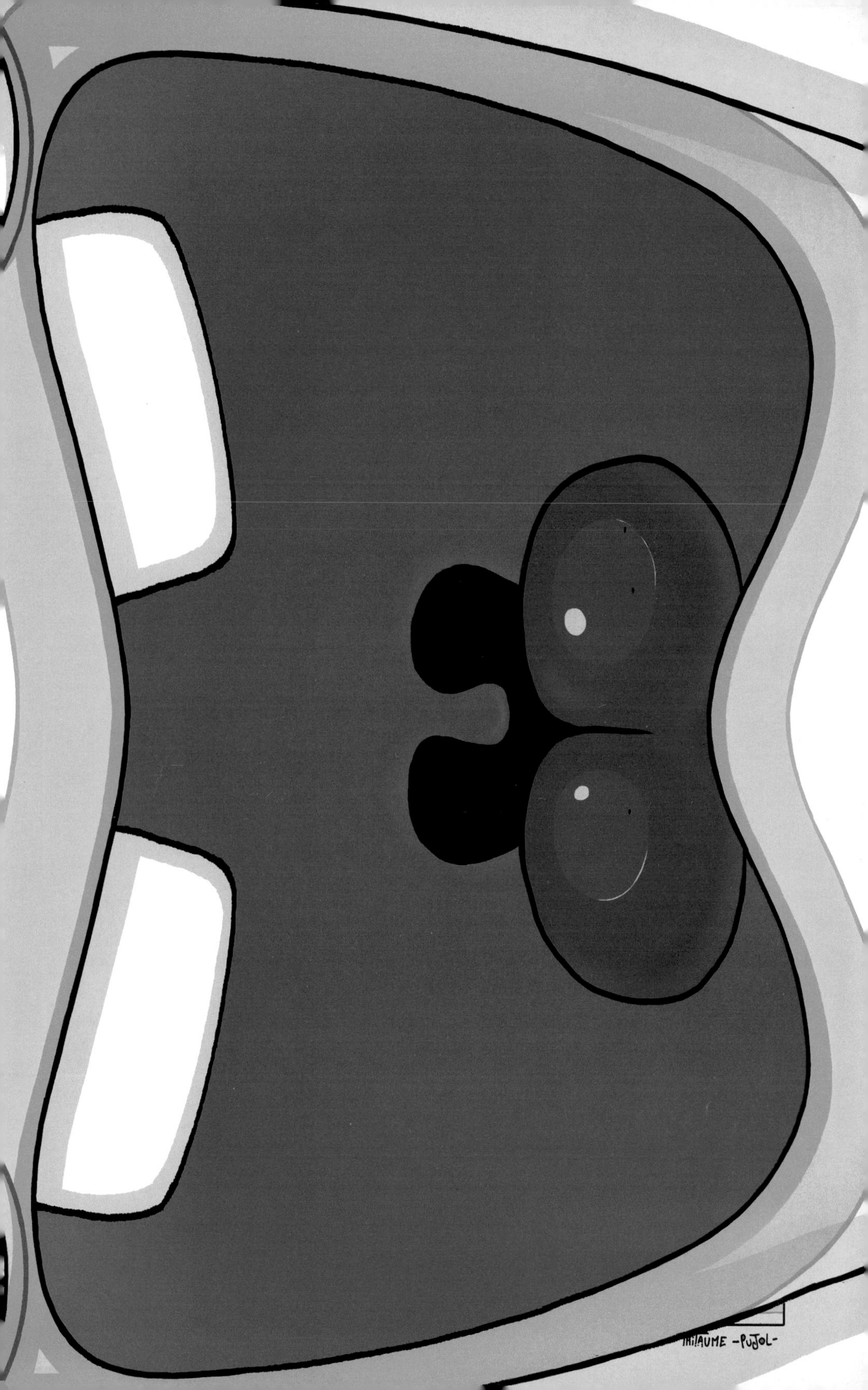
-PUJOL-

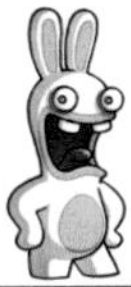

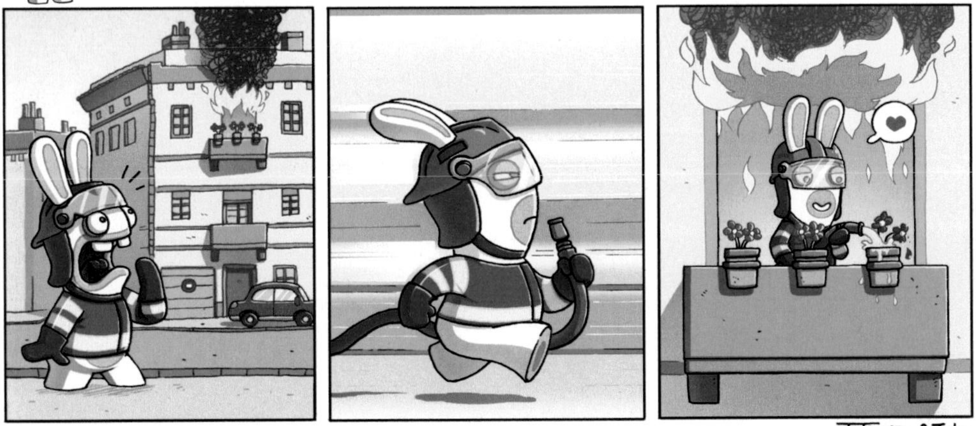

THITAUME -PUJOL-

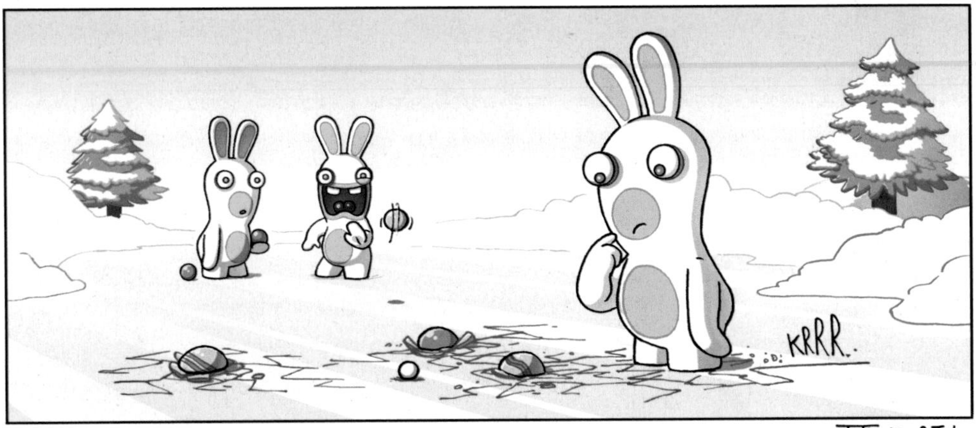
KRRR.

THITAUME -PUJOL-

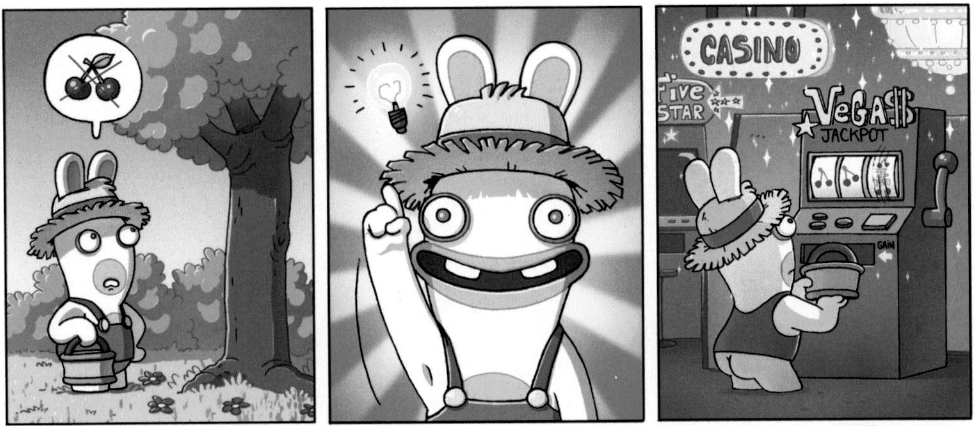
CASINO
Five STAR
VEGAS
JACKPOT
GAIN

THITAUME -PUJOL-

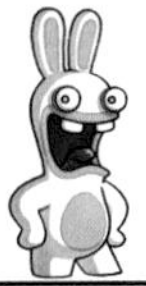

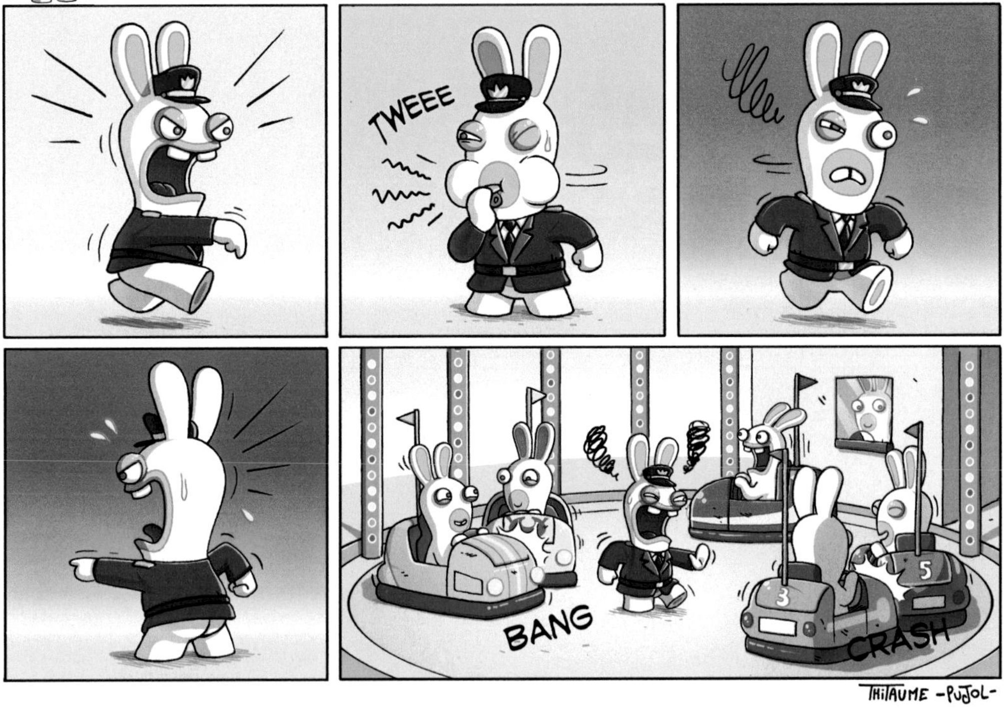
TWEEE
BANG
CRASH
THITAUME -PUJOL-

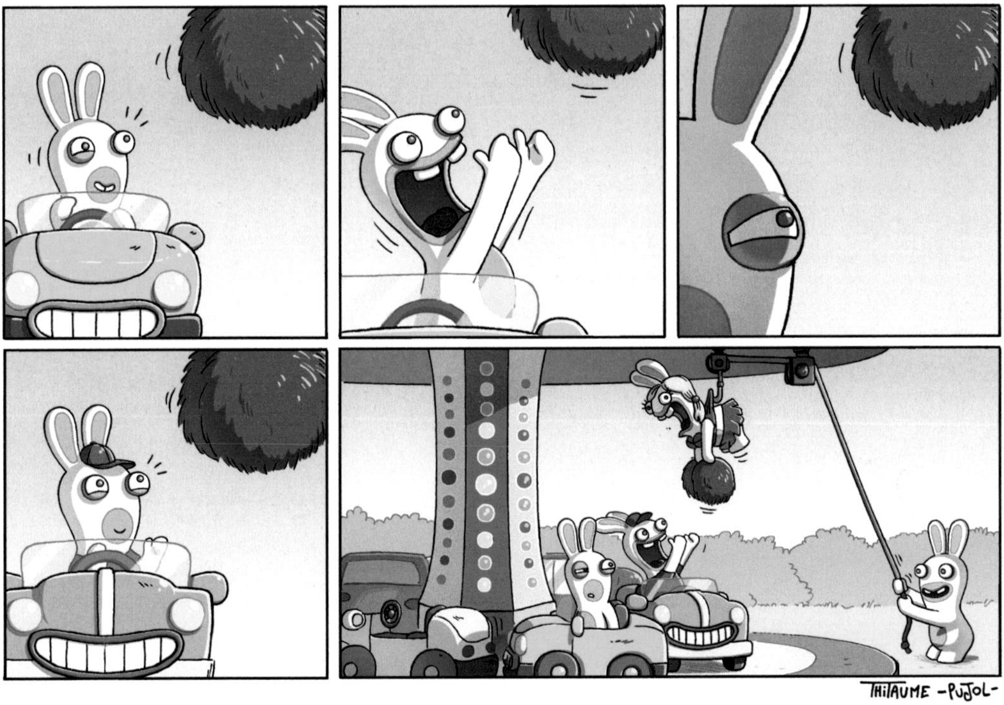
THITAUME -PUJOL-

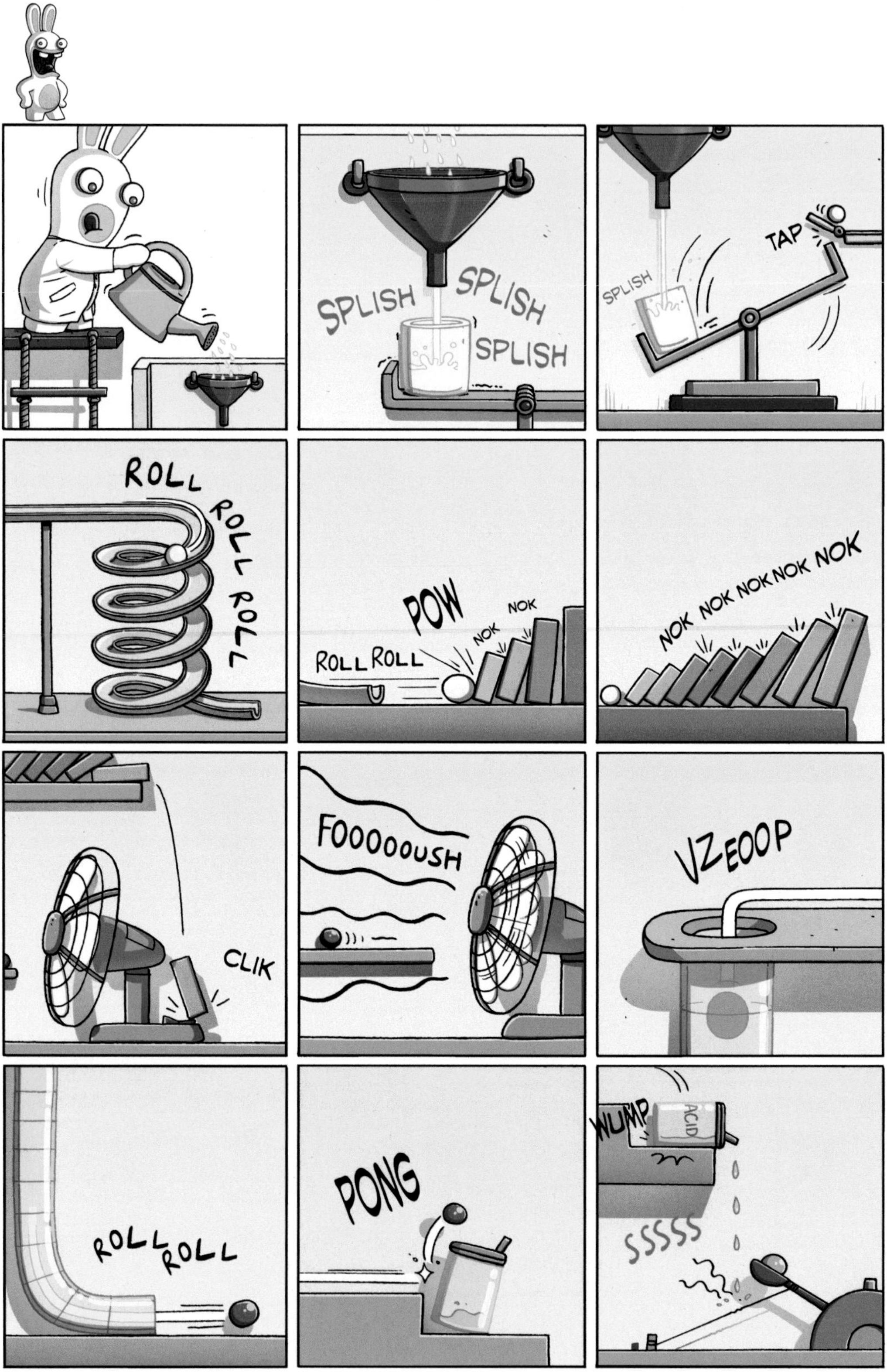
SPLISH
SPLISH
SPLISH
SPLISH
TAP
ROLL
ROLL
ROLL
ROLL
POW
ROLL ROLL
NOK
NOK
NOK NOK NOK NOK NOK NOK
CLIK
FOOOOOUSH
VZEOOP
ROLL ROLL
PONG
WUMP
ACID
SSSSS

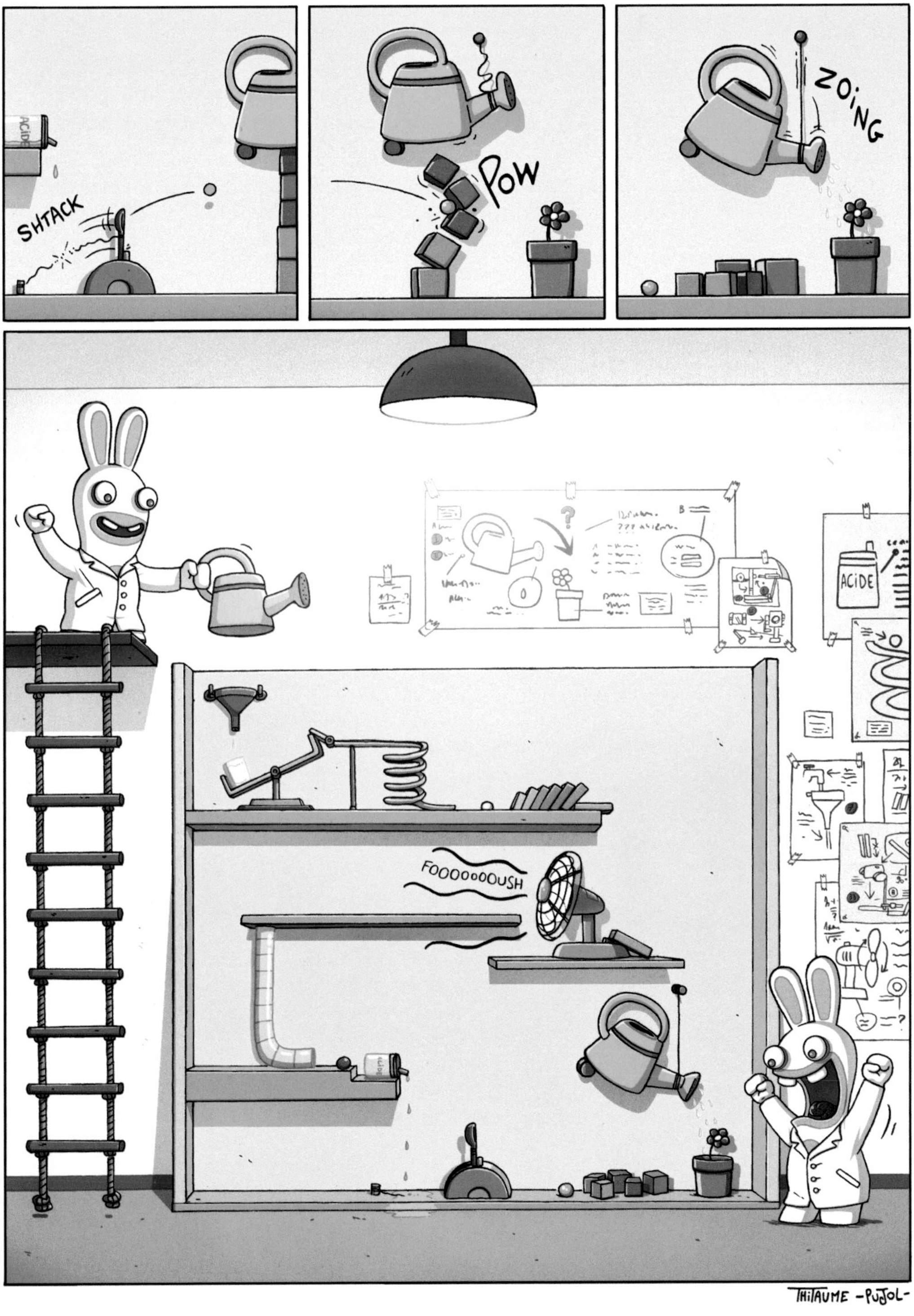

ACIDE
SHTACK
POW
ZOING
ACIDE
FOOOOOOOUSH
THITAUME -PUJOL-

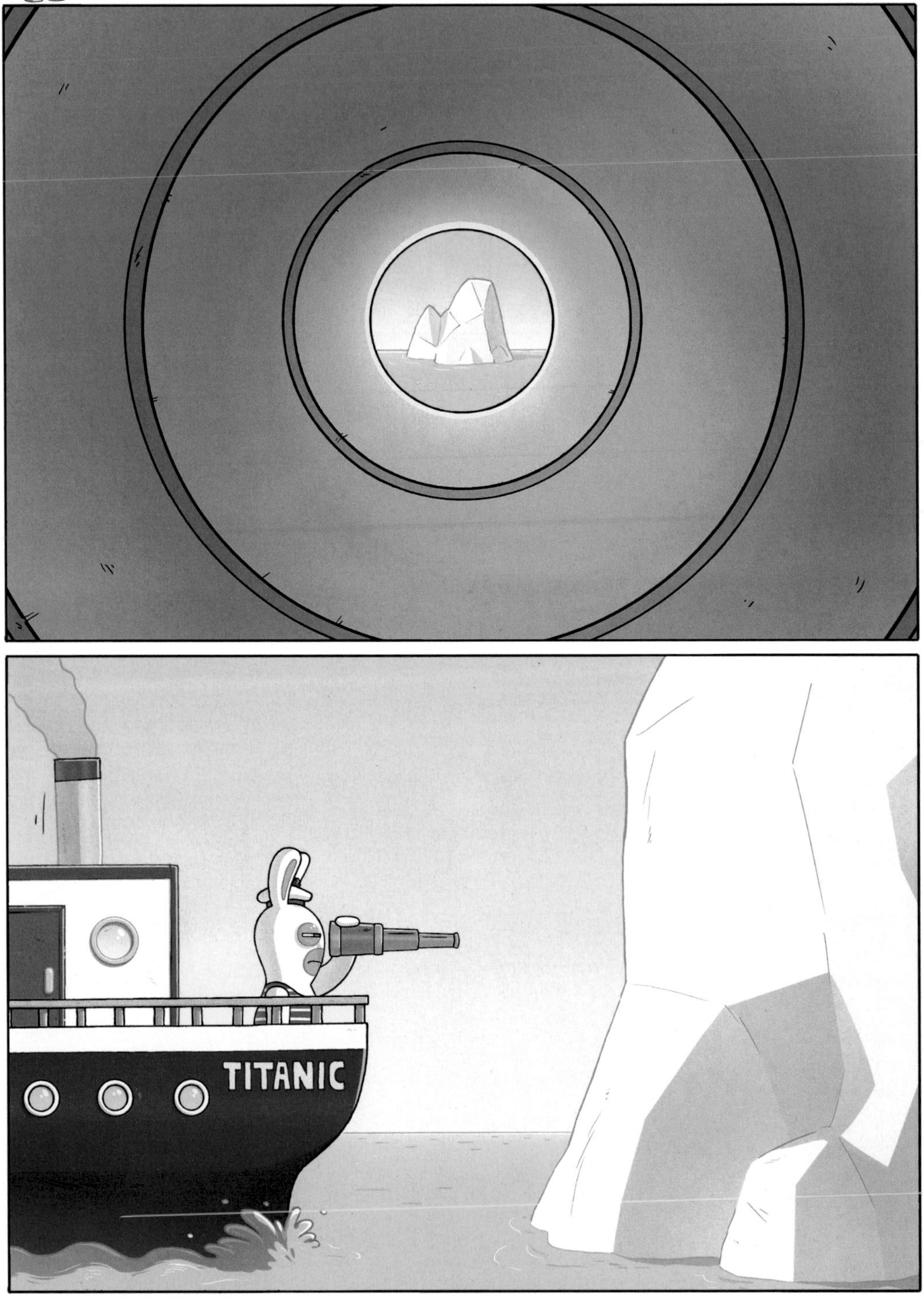
TITANIC

THITAUME -PUJOL-

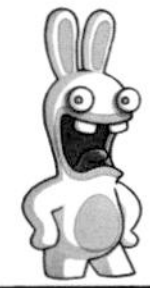

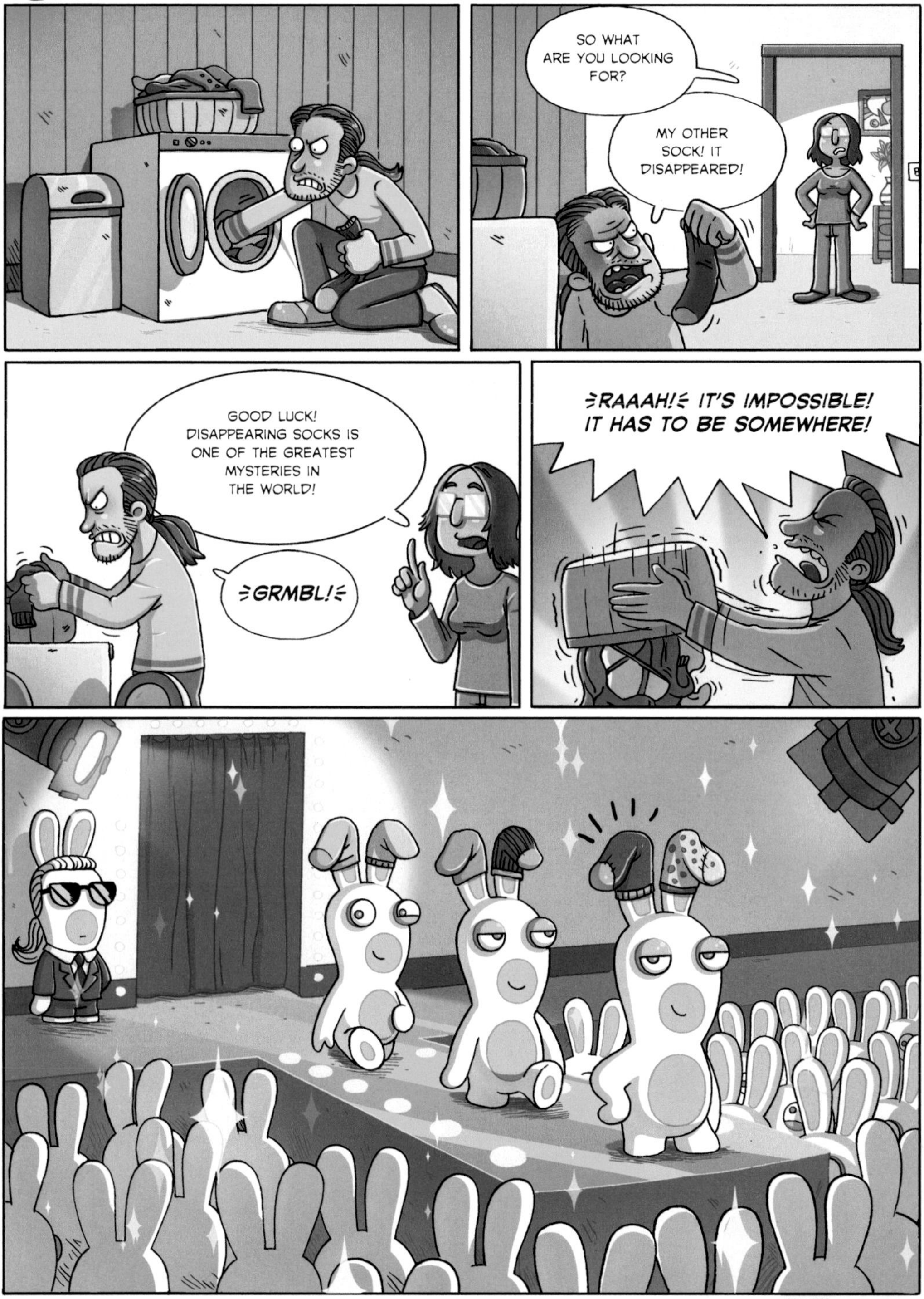
SO WHAT ARE YOU LOOKING FOR?
MY OTHER SOCK! IT DISAPPEARED!
GOOD LUCK! DISAPPEARING SOCKS IS ONE OF THE GREATEST MYSTERIES IN THE WORLD!
GRMBL!
RAAAH! IT'S IMPOSSIBLE! IT HAS TO BE SOMEWHERE!

THiLAUME -PUJOL-

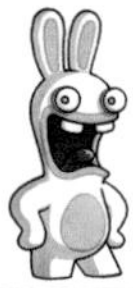

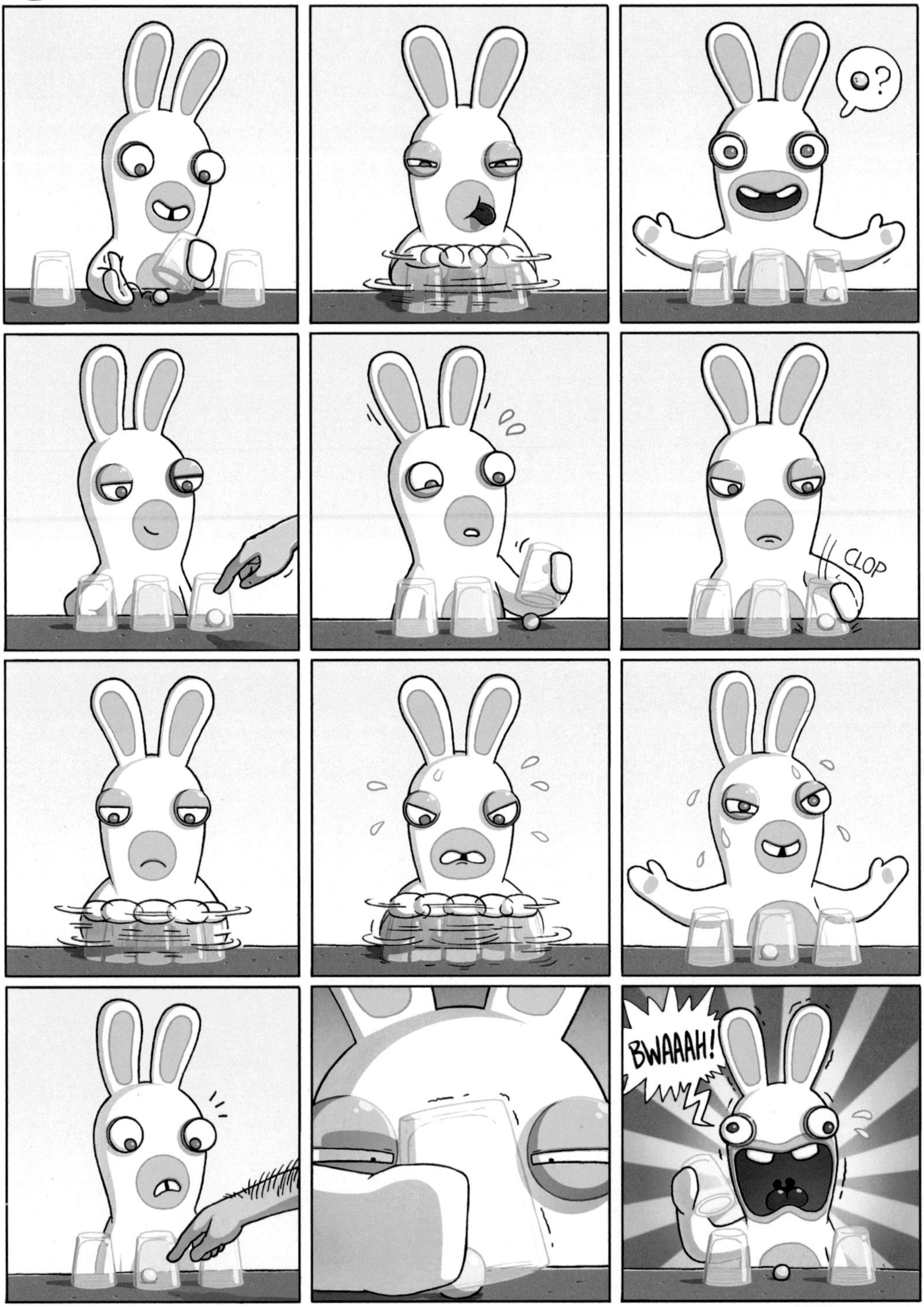

?
CLOP
BWAAAH!
THiTAUME -PUJOL-

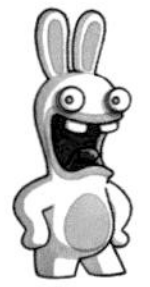

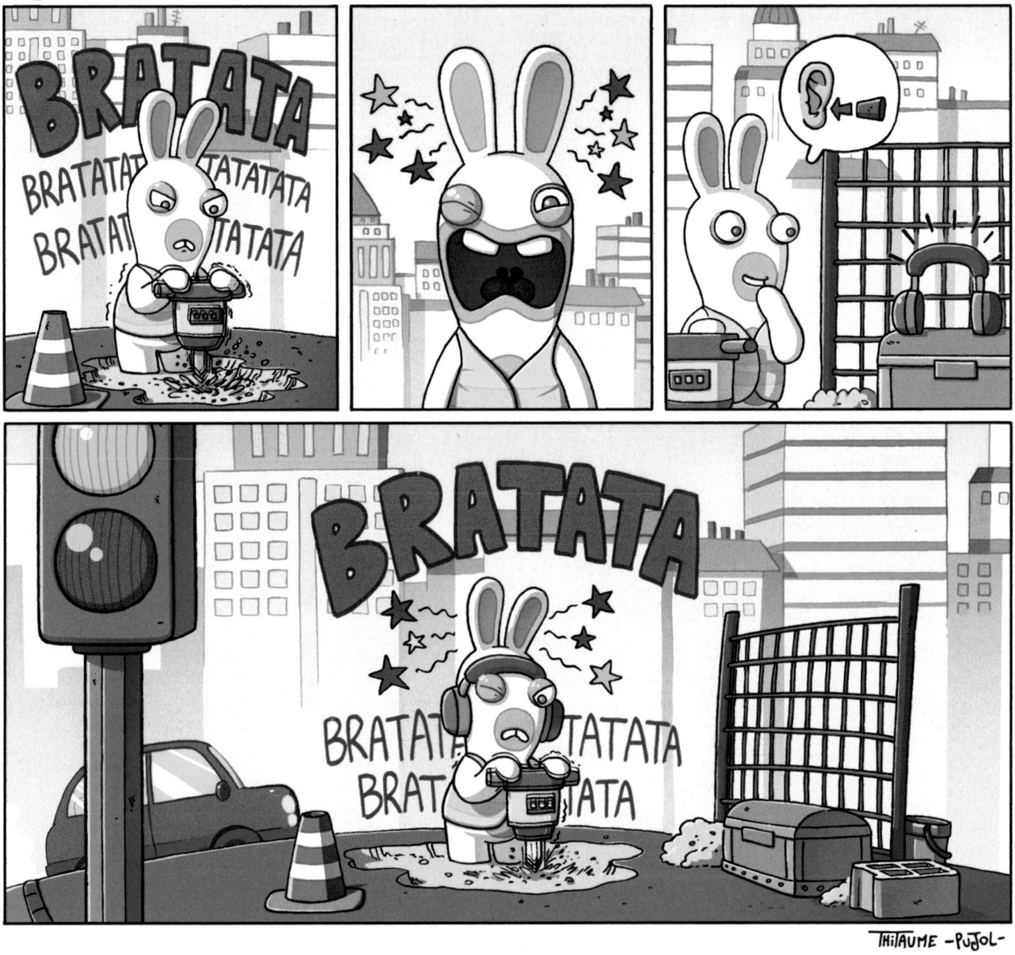
BRATATA
BRATATAT TATATATA
BRATAT TATATA
BRATATA
BRATATA TATATA
BRAT TATA
THITAUME -PUJOL-

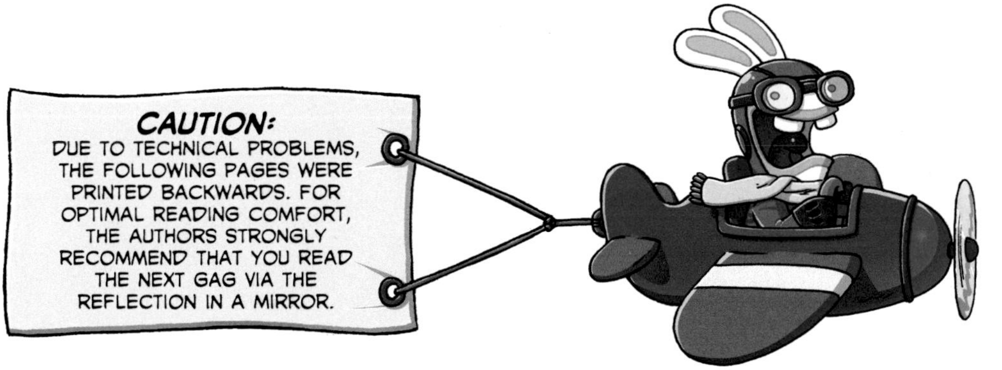
CAUTION:
DUE TO TECHNICAL PROBLEMS, THE FOLLOWING PAGES WERE PRINTED BACKWARDS. FOR OPTIMAL READING COMFORT, THE AUTHORS STRONGLY RECOMMEND THAT YOU READ THE NEXT GAG VIA THE REFLECTION IN A MIRROR.

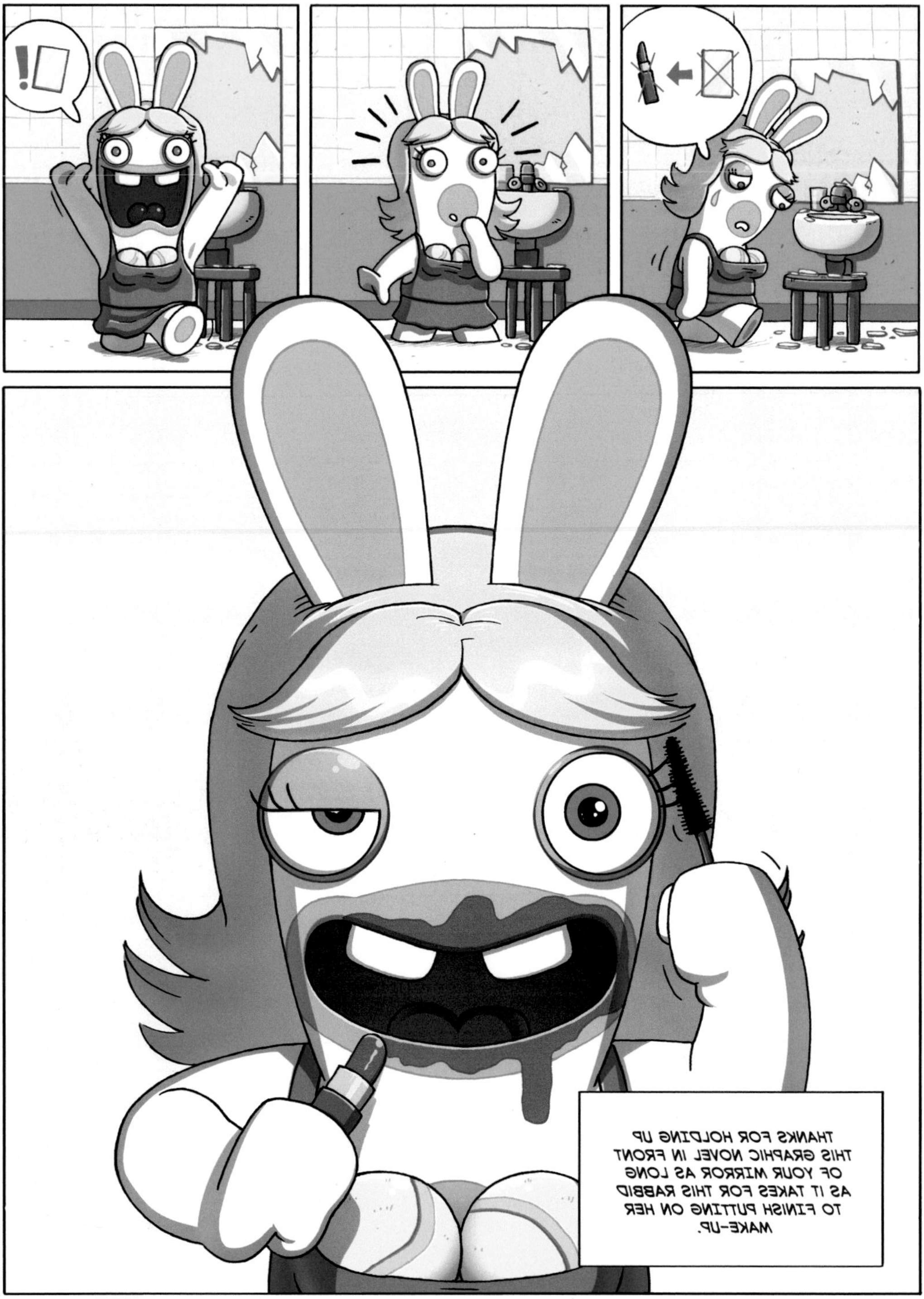
THANKS FOR HOLDING UP THIS GRAPHIC NOVEL IN FRONT OF YOUR MIRROR AS LONG AS IT TAKES FOR THIS RABBID TO FINISH PUTTING ON HER MAKE-UP.
THITAUME -PUJOL-

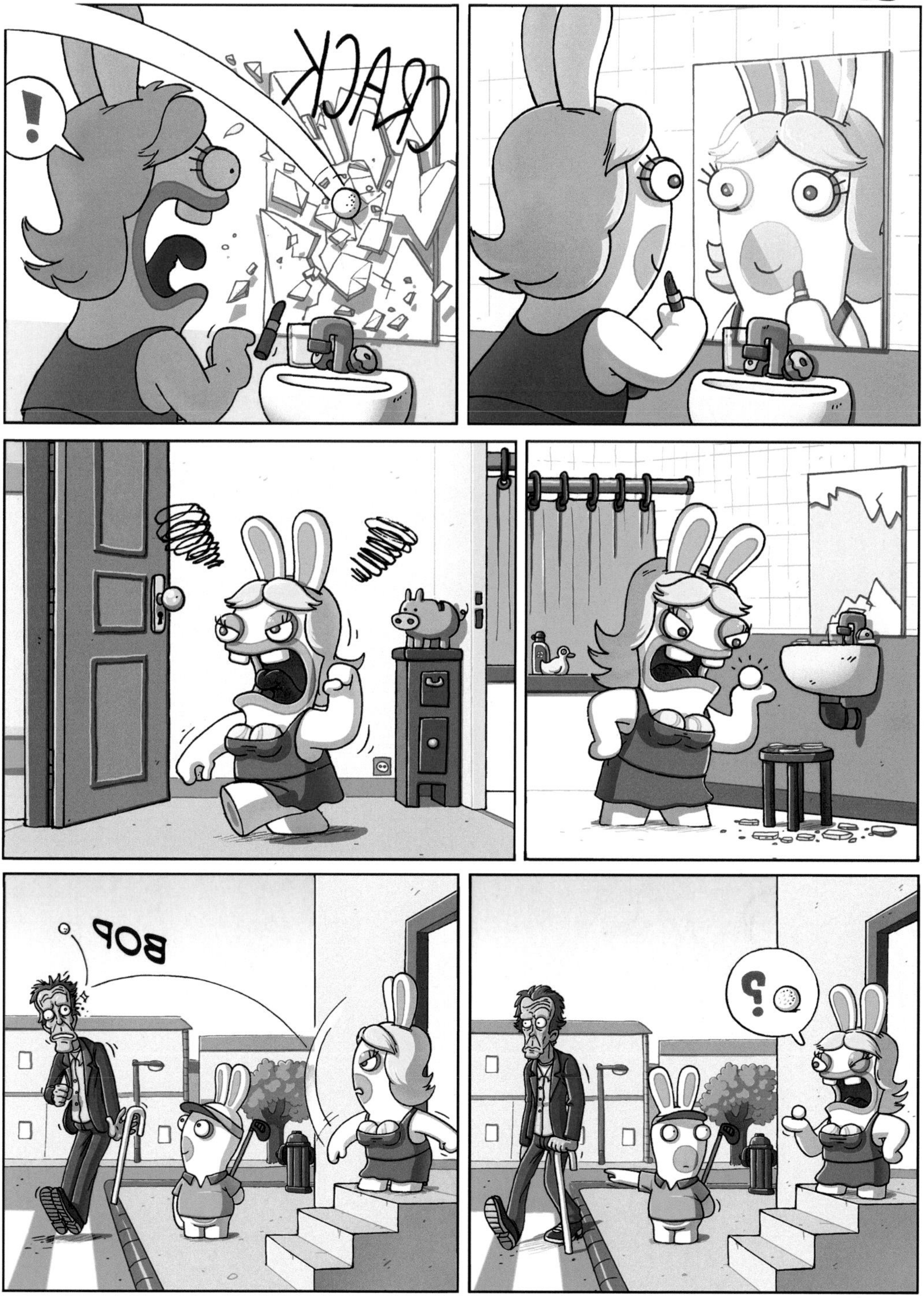
!
CRACK
BOP
?

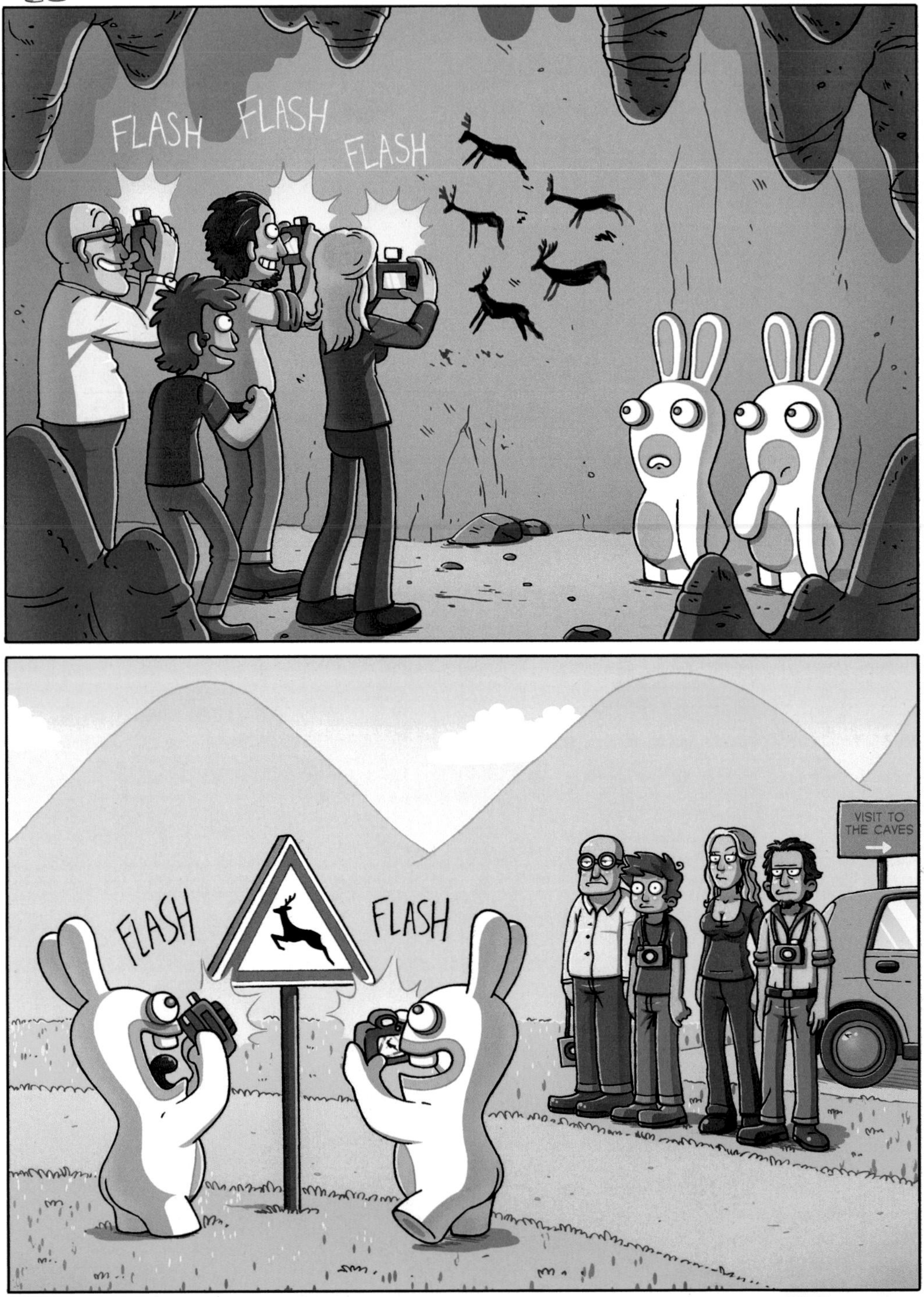
FLASH
FLASH
FLASH
FLASH
FLASH
VISIT TO THE CAVES
THITAUME -PUJOL-

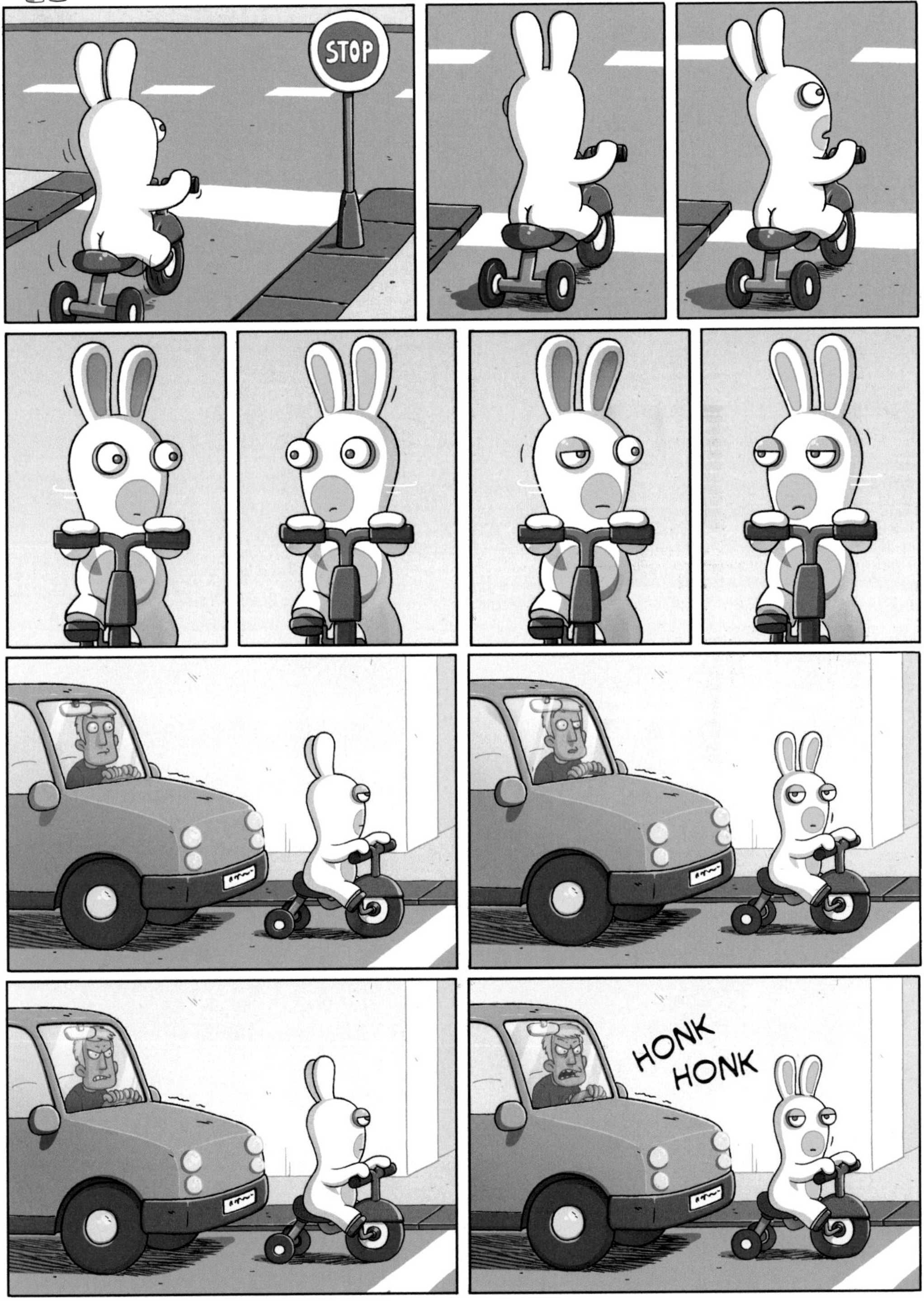
STOP
HONK
HONK

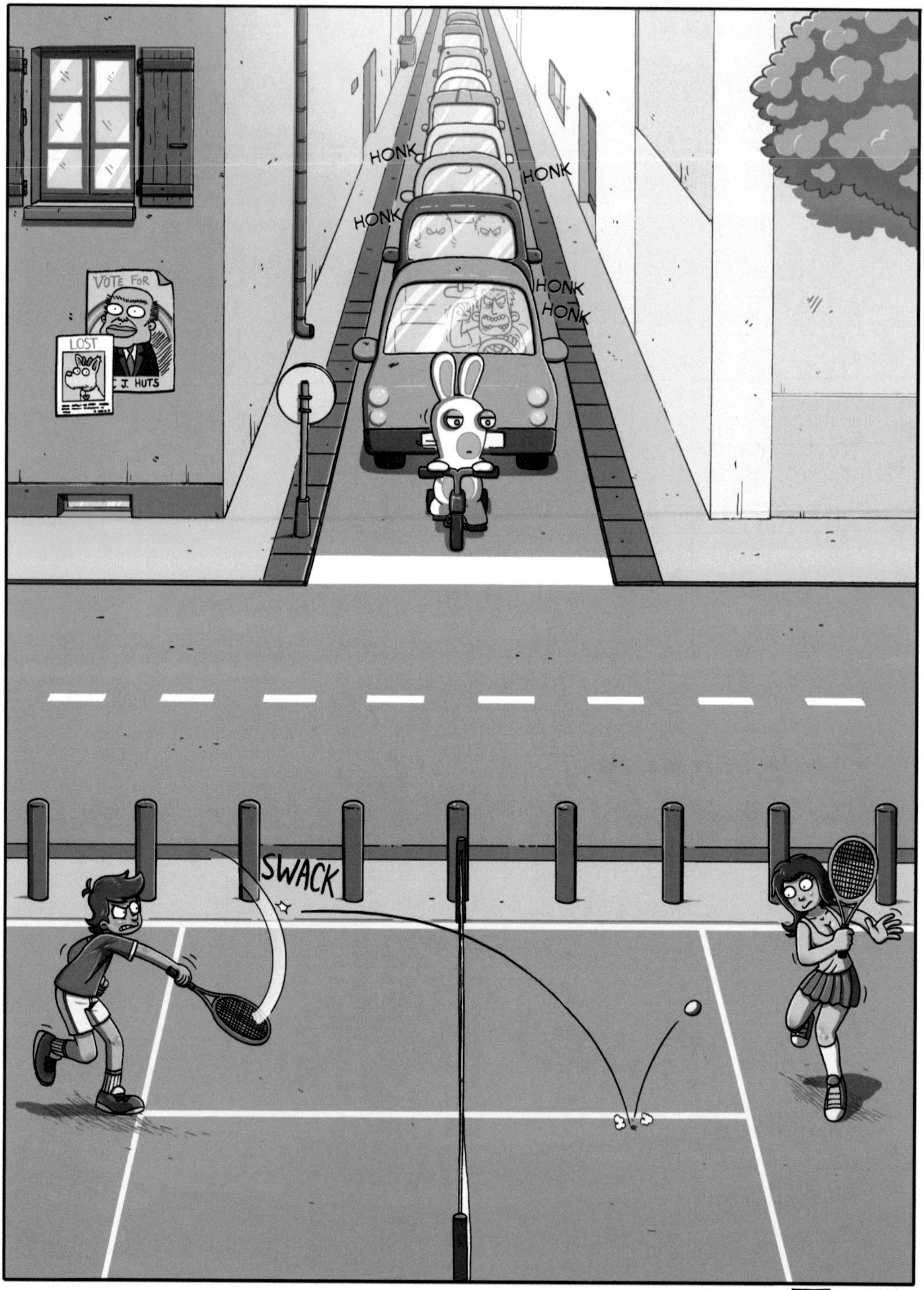
HONK
HONK
HONK
HONK
HONK
VOTE FOR
LOST
C J. HUTS
SWACK

THITAUME -PUJOL-

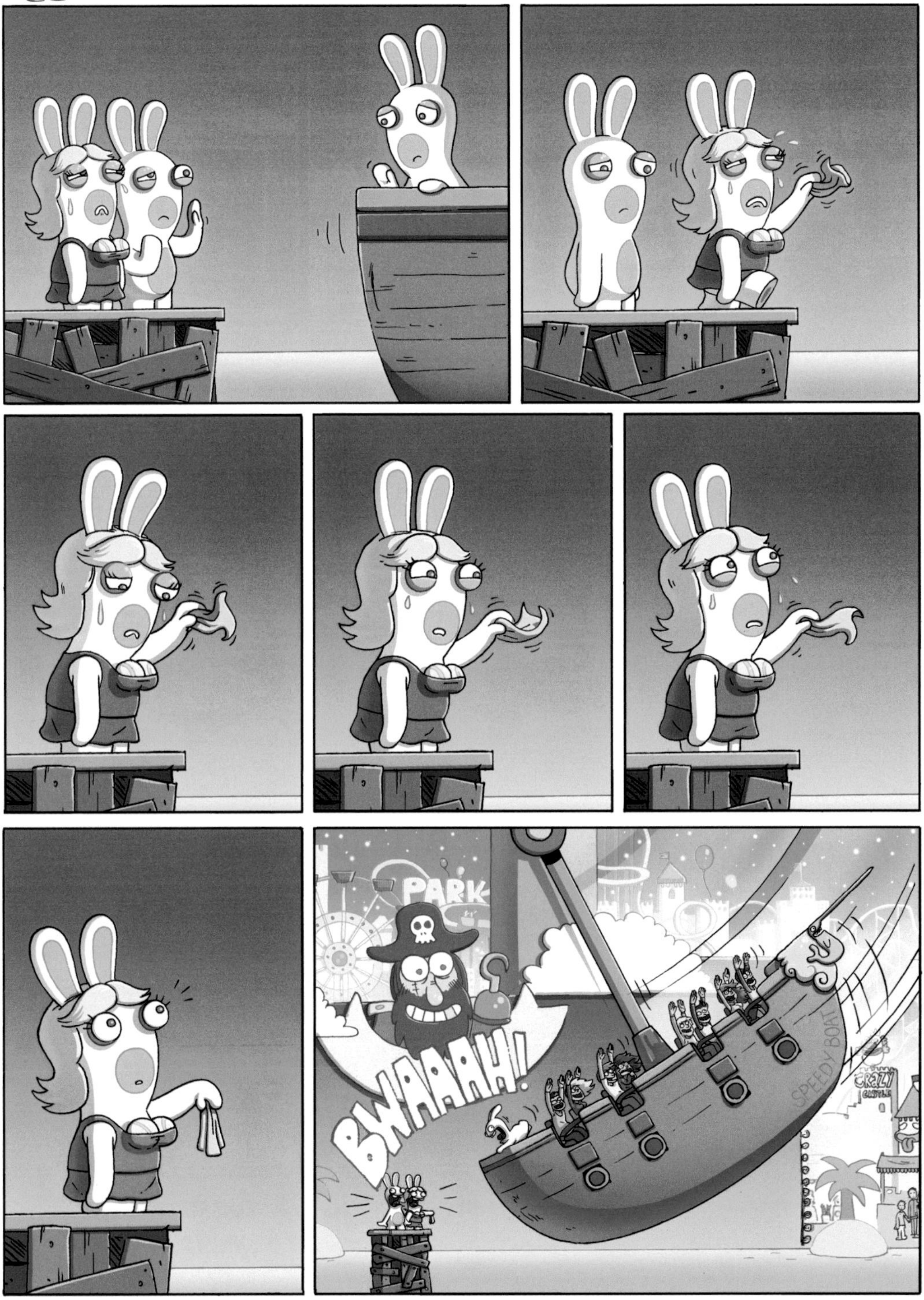
PARK
BWAAAAH!!
SPEEDY BOAT
CRAZY CASTLE

THITAUME -PUJOL-

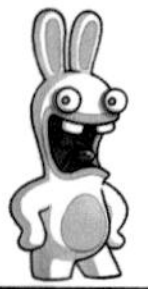

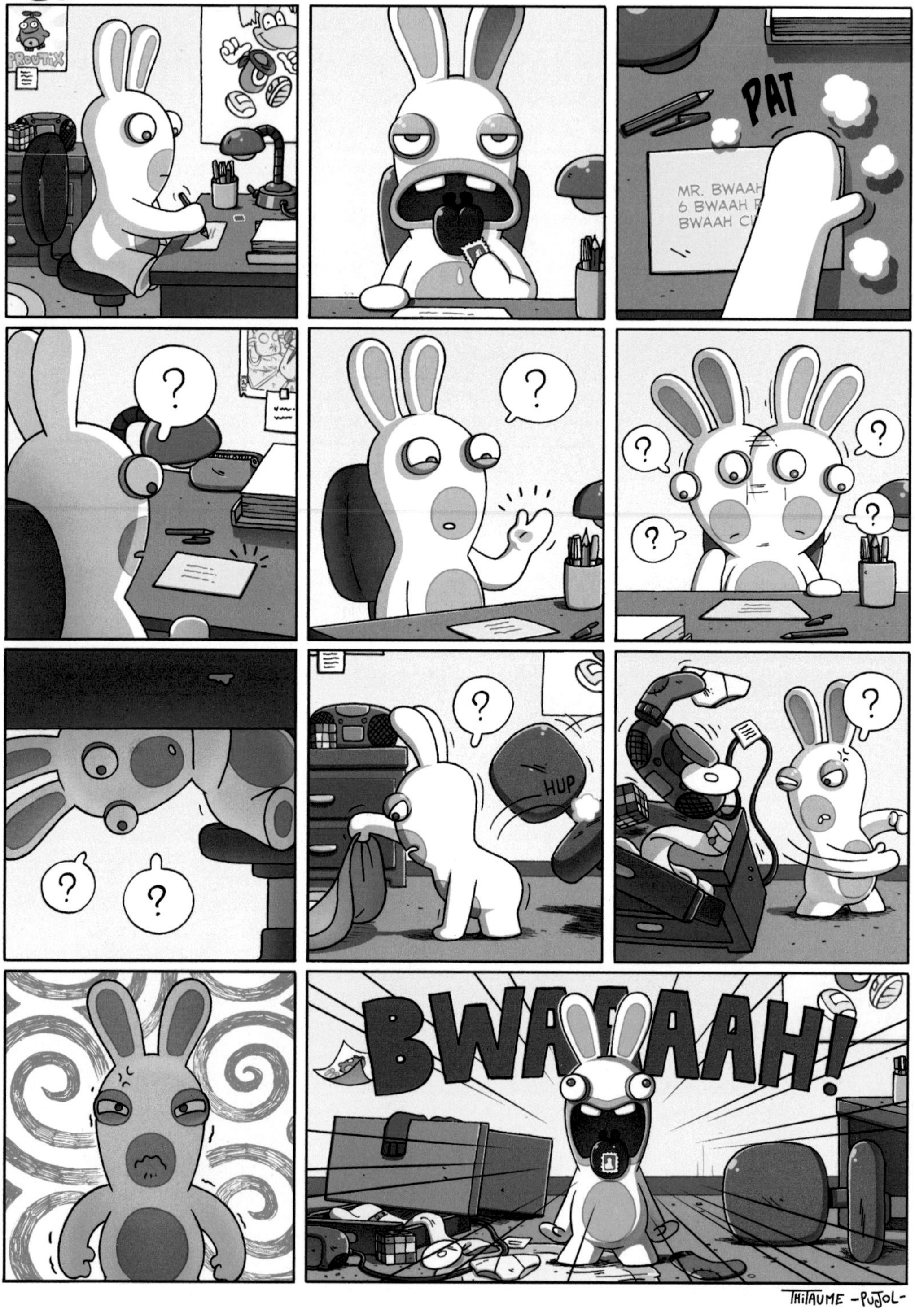
PROUTIX
PAT
MR. BWAAH
6. BWAAH
BWAAH C
?
?
?
?
?
?
?
?
?
HUP
?
BWA AAH!

THITAUME -PUJOL-

THITAUME -PUJOL-

THiTAUME -PuJoL-

THiTAUME -PuJoL-

THi

FLASH

THITAUME -PUJOL-

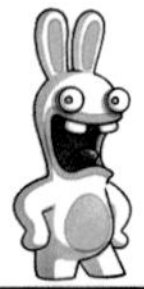
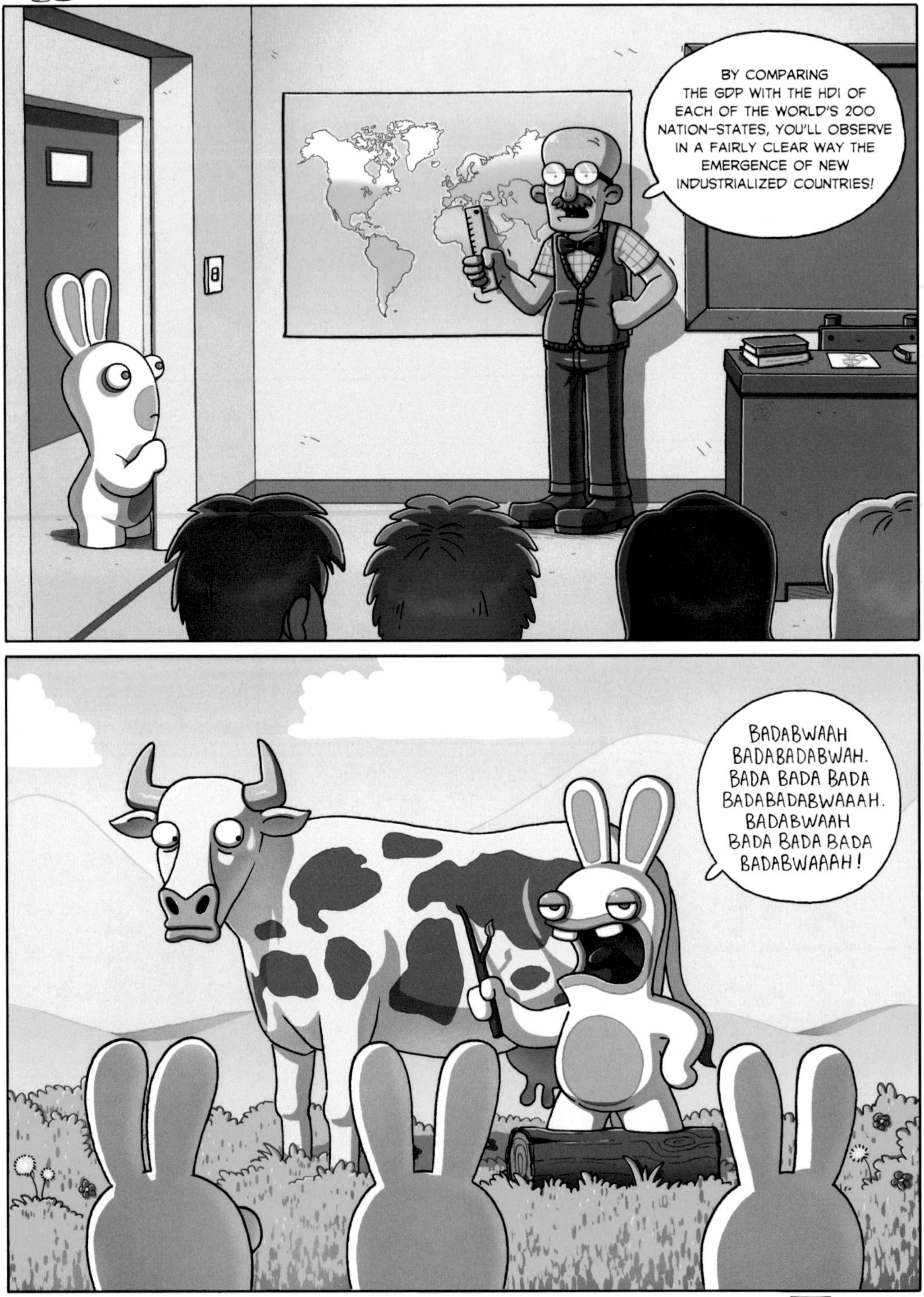
BY COMPARING THE GDP WITH THE HDI OF EACH OF THE WORLD'S 200 NATION-STATES, YOU'LL OBSERVE IN A FAIRLY CLEAR WAY THE EMERGENCE OF NEW INDUSTRIALIZED COUNTRIES!
BADABWAAH BADABADABWAH. BADA BADA BADA BADABADABWAAAH. BADABWAAH BADA BADA BADA BADABWAAAH!
THITAUME -PUJOL-

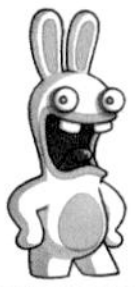

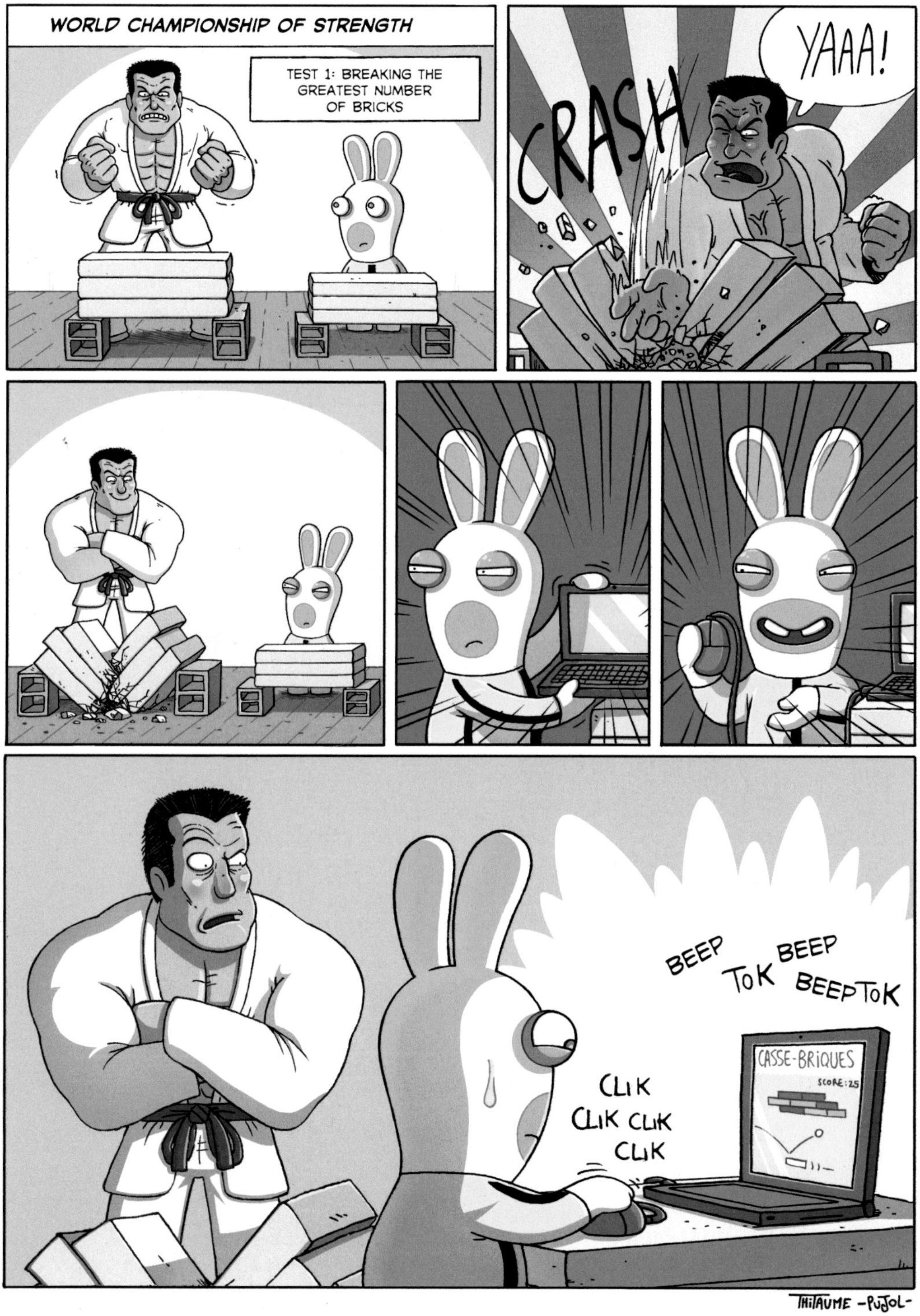
WORLD CHAMPIONSHIP OF STRENGTH
TEST 1: BREAKING THE GREATEST NUMBER OF BRICKS
CRASH
YAAA!
BEEP
TOK BEEP
BEEPTOK
CLIK
CLIK CLIK
CLIK
CASSE-BRIQUES
SCORE: 25
THITAUME -PUJOL-

SOLUTIONS TO THE BIG BONUS GAME

Here's where the hidden objects are located:

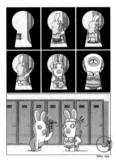

Page 7 : the dentures

HAPPY NEW YEAR
BWAAAH!

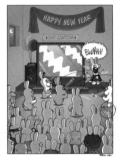

Page 10 : the flippers

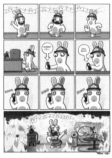

Page 15 : the pair of glasses

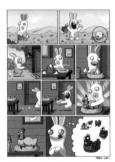

Page 17 : the balloon

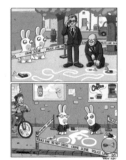

Page 22: the horn

TITANIC

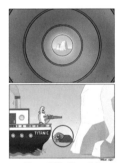

Page 38: the pink elephant

FLASH
FLASH

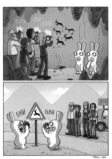

Page 44: the mechanical monkey

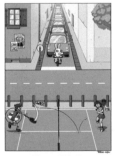

Page 46: the life preserver

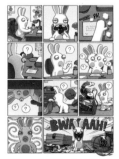

Page 48: the bagpipes

WATCH OUT FOR PAPERCUTZ

Welcome to the super-silly second RABBIDS graphic novel, by Thitaume, Romain Pujol, and Gorobei, from Papercutz—those semi-humorous humans dedicated to publishing great graphic novels for all ages. I'm Jim Salicrup, the enthusiastic Editor-in-Chief, who likes to fill up a page in each and every Papercutz graphic novel so you can be better acquainted with me and the folks that put these books together. Somehow, this page didn't make it into the premiere RABBIDS graphic novel, so we've got a lot to do! We're going to use this page to alert you to our second graphic novel, and...

A BIG THANKS TO OUR SPONSOR

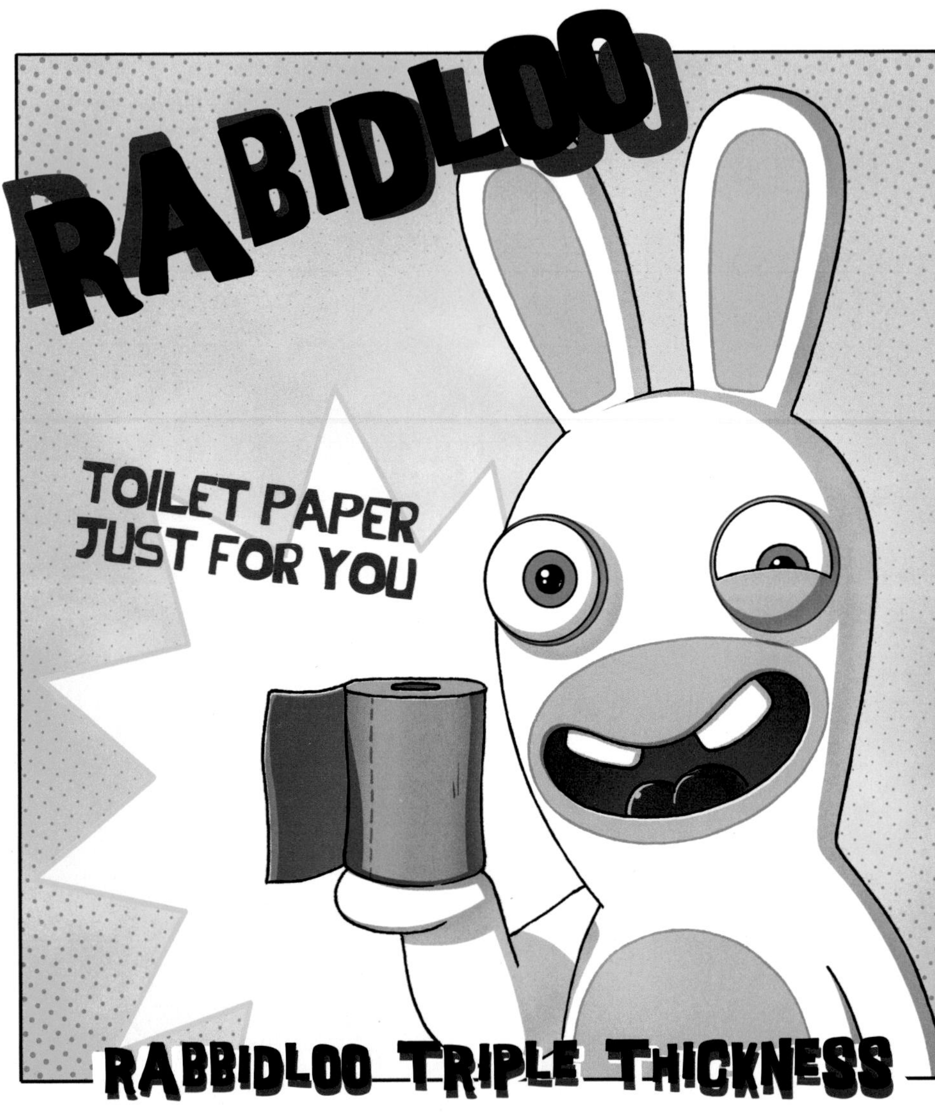
RABIDLOO
TOILET PAPER JUST FOR YOU
RABBIDLOO TRIPLE THICKNESS

THANKS TO THE REVOLUTIONARY TECHNOLOGY OF THE RABBIDLOO FACTORIES, THIS BOOK WAS PRINTED ENTIRELY ON RECYCLED TOILET PAPER!

DESPITE EXTREMELY RIGOROUS SAFETY TESTING, THE NATIONAL HEALTH AND HYGIENE AGENCY RECOMMENDS YOU WASH YOUR HANDS AFTER EACH USE OF THIS BOOK.